BANSHEE
FIRES OF REVENGE
by Billy Young

Published by Lulu.com
ISBN 978 1 4475 2589 9
First Edition

All characters, events and ghosts are fictional. Any resemblance to any real people or events is purely a coincidence.

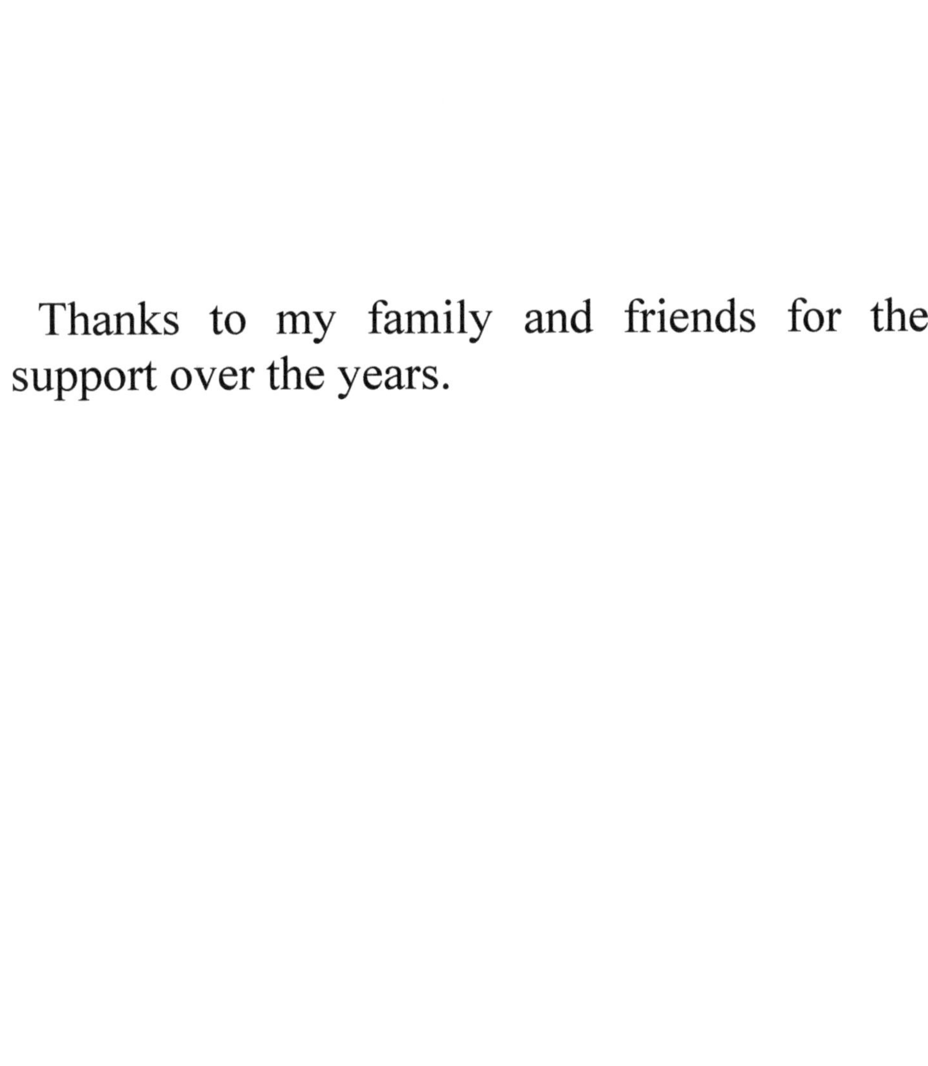

Thanks to my family and friends for the support over the years.

Other book by Billy Young:

A Winter Journey
Banshee Angel of Judgement
Bublos
Teddy the Bear

Chapter 1

Detective John Munroe scanned the faces of the mourners, ticking off each as he recognised them. His gaze fell on someone he hadn't met before. She was an older woman, stout but not overweight. Her hair was white with the passing of years and her face showed the lined weathering of time. She had to be related to the grieving family for she stood within the select group, seemingly trying to comfort the grandmother. Just as other members of the clan were comforting the mother who was standing on the grandmother's other side. Maybe an old friend of the distraught woman, he thought on guessing they had to be about the same age. Or at least not too far apart.

"Let us now bow our head in a moment of quiet contemplation and remember Micky and how he brought light into our lives. How when we felt down, he was there to lend an ear," the clergyman said his voice droned with little emotion. The crowd did as they were asked, the grey sky adding to the sad scene in the new extension to the old cemetery. A tall Victorian brick wall separated the older part from the one time farmer's field, which now served for new graves.

Munroe was not the only one not bow his head, as the light rain slowly worked its way into his marrow. Susie Mclean a reporter for a local paper stared back across at him. He glanced away at the neat rows laid out to allow the dead their rest. He hadn't needed to come to the funeral, but wished to show the family that though the police were lost to why Micky and his friend had lost their lives, he was still interested in the case. He wasn't sure how he would find answers, yet he felt there was more to the case. After all there was the history of the old cottage where the lads had met their end.

He didn't believe that it was the ghost that was said to haunt the dwelling, as Allan Ferris had tried hard to convince him a week earlier. Ferris had claimed to have information, so like a rookie he had fallen into the trap of seeing him. Uniform had conveniently not mentioned they knew the man was a bit of a local character, and ghost freak. Since then it had become a bit of a joke even in CID.

Yet still the case didn't settle well with him. Maybe it's just that the older lad died of nothing, he thought, remembering how the autopsy had found no cause of death. In the end the coroner had put down heart failure, though he had told Munroe that this was simply so he didn't have to put unexplained on the death certificate. "Best for the family don't you think, rather than have it all hanging over them with no answers," had been Winters', the coroner, explanation.

Why had the lads' been running through the woods? What had or who had driven them to head away from home? Munroe had no answers and it bothered him. He liked everything in a neat bundle, packaged away and explainable. It helped in his job, it helped him keep a detachment, which was needed sometimes.

As the gathered bereaved raised their heads, Munroe felt an awkward moment as the woman he had been gazing at before the prayers, caught his eye. She whispered something to the grandmother next to her but continued to stare at him.

* * *

Mandy raised her head sensing the clergyman was about to sum up. So the mourners could make their way to the gathering place in a Lyndon Castle to show their support for the family. She noticed a man standing at the back of the crowd opposite watching her. "Who's that?" she whispered under her breath to her sister keeping her gaze fixed on him with suspicion.

"He's a policeman, Munroe or something like that." The woman remembered meeting him briefly but had more important things, at the time on her mind to take much notice of him.

"You haven't told him about me?" Mandy said hastily, not wanting anything to do with the questions that he may have.

"What? No, why would I?" She looked at Mandy wondering why she seemed worried. "It's not like you remember anything from back then, right?" Alice tried to dismiss it,

"You act like you're wanted or something. You aren't are you?"

"No," Mandy didn't want to remember the cottage but her nephew's death had brought back the nightmare she knew existed there. This made her nervous and afraid as the old nightmares returned to haunt the dark hours. "Well, maybe I do remember something but this isn't the place or time."

"What do you mean?" The grandmother felt a dread in her soul for she knew whatever Mandy remember would have a bearing on what had happened to the grandson.

"Not here," Mandy sounded mysterious, "we can talk later."

"Dust to dust," the clergyman's words brought an end to the proceedings and the conversation before the matter could be pressed.

As the crowd began to make their way towards the small parking space they stopped to say their condolences to the family. First talking in hushed tones to Mandy's niece before saying how sorry they were to her sister. She was glad to be mostly ignored by the mourners.

Mandy kept her eye on the policeman, hoping he wouldn't come forwards and was glad to see he didn't. The last thing she wanted was his probing into her private life or what she might know about the cottage. Even though she had left Scotland after her escape from the ghost that lived there, she still felt unease at being back in the area. This was as close as she wanted to be to the cottage, yet knew that she might have to overcome her fear of it. After all she couldn't let it claim any more lives, it had done enough damage to her family already.

She rubbed at the sleeve of her coat and the scars it hide beneath. Her mind filled with the memory of the night she had come face to face with the nightmare that had chased her ever since. The screaming phantom that had taken her friends' lives, her boyfriend's life and she had barely escaped from. She was sure that it had been this evil apparition that had taken her sister's grandson.

Over the years Mandy had lost touch with her family. Only the internet had managed to reconnect her with her sister. She regretted that she had never gotten to her parents funeral or even heard of their passing until she became linked up to the big wide web. So much time and so much running only to end up back at the beginning, she mused to herself with a shudder.

Life hadn't been bad all of the time though. She had been married for over twenty years, though with no kids to complete it. Sadly Alfred had passed away quietly two years ago. It was only then that her mind turned to the family she had lost touch with, and so she had began searching the net, unsure whether she could trace them. She was shocked to find it easier to track them down than she had thought, even more so to find that her sister still lived in New Mills.

"Yes, we're having the reception at Lyndon Castle," one of Mandy's cousin's was saying to another man bringing her from her internal thoughts.

"Do you need a lift Mandy?" Her cousin asked already knowing she had shared the main car with Alice, her sister but felt she just had to check.

"I'm fine," she said, it almost whispered, "I'll see you there."

She gave Alice a hug before making their way to the car. Maybe I should have come back sooner to end this, she thought. She knew though that it was the fear that had held her back. She felt it in the pit of her stomach as she opened the car door. The prospect of heading closer to the source of that fear niggled at the back of her mind. At the same time she was worried about what she had to tell her sister. How will she take it? Was the pressing thought as Alice climbed in behind her. She pushed it, like everything else, out of her head. She also hoped that Alice wouldn't try to press on her earlier slip of the tongue.

* * *

As Susie followed the rest of the crowd towards the car park she asked the man that had been standing near her who the woman was.

"Who?" he answered her with a questioning looking. "Oh, that would be Mandy, Alice's sister. I'm surprised to see her though, I thought she had died years ago. She left, you see, after what happened to her boyfriend back in sixty eight."

"And what did happen?" Susie felt a creeping thrill at learning something new about the family, sure it may have a bearing on the story in some way.

"Oh, they were those hippies that OD'd in the cottage in the woods back then. Strange how her great nephew died there as well?"

"Oh, yes of course," she pretended to know all about it but made a mental note to check up on the story later. The man nodded and then headed for his lift to the free drinks and Susie made for her's to head to the office for some internet searching.

* * *

Munroe watched as the mourners slowly left. He felt like he should offer his sympathies but didn't wish to intrude any more than he had already. He wasn't even meant to be there, yet had found himself drawn to the graveyard. His thoughts were on the mystery woman, who was she and what relation was she to the family? He had thought he had met all the family over the past few weeks since the discovery of the strange deaths. The woman seemed strangely familiar but he couldn't place her. He was sure though he had never had the pleasure of meeting her before.

As the last car drew out of the car park he finally began to make his way to his own. His thoughts still trying hard to place the woman. He was usually very good at remembering faces, yet she seemed to elude him. Maybe its just she looks so like Alice, he thought in an attempt to dismiss the brain racking he knew he would go through till he found an answer. He knew it didn't matter anyway as he had been told to drop the case as there appeared to be nothing suspicious in the two deaths or so his commanding officer would have it. He didn't agree, any unexplained deaths were worthy of investigating to him.

Chapter 2

Mandy had been unsure of coming to the wake as it was being held at Lyndon Castle. It was far to close to the place of all her troubles, the place where it had all begun, haunting her through the years. In the end though she knew she had to go. If for no other reason than to show her support to her sister and family. But she had another reason, a more important one.

She knew why her nephew had died, she knew what dwelled in the cottage in the woods. And in away she felt that it was in some way her fault, after all she had remained silent for too long about what she knew of that cottage, about the creature that was tied to that house. Guilt at surviving, fear of what others would say had prevented her telling her tale. Even her late husband had never known the truth of the nightmares. Instead she had always found a way to dismiss them to him.

Now the same evil had risen again to take more lives. She was unsure how to approach the subject with Alice and as the guest slowly began to thin she knew she would have to make her move soon. Still, though she had rehearsed it in her head, her fear of causing greater distress held her back.

“I’d love a cup of tea.” Alice said. She was seated across the table from Mandy.

Mandy had been amazed that the old manor house and grounds had been turned into a theme park come hotel. “I’m sure they’d get a pot for you if you asked,” Mandy said, turning to look for a waitress.

“No, I can wait till I get home,” Alice said dismissively, “I’ll enjoy it more and I can take these blasted shoes off.”

“Why not kick them off under the table.”

“I don’t think I’d get them back on,” she said, moving uncomfortably in her chair, a painful smile filling her face. “I should have broken them in but with everything else there wasn’t the time.”

A tall figure appeared at the table. The well dress woman with mousy coloured hair smiled gently at Alice as she spoke, “I don’t know if you remember me from my visit to your daughter's." Her accent showed she wasn't local. Mandy thought she sounded southern English.

"Yes, you're the manager or something for the park?" Alice was sure she was right but still felt the need to ask.

"Yes, the Rides Manager," she said rather self importantly, "I just wished to offer the park's condolences. Micky, though he only worked with us for a short time, was a valued member of our little family here." The woman's eyes showed false sympathy, as if she had donned a mask for this occasion.

"That is very kind, thank you." Alice felt a lump in her throat, wishing the woman had not reminded her of why she was here. After all there was little need, as how could she ever forget. And how was it such a short time, she thought studying the woman's hairy top lip, he worked here on and off for years.

"It was such a tragedy and we all felt his loss at the park," the woman added, looking awkward as a moments silence opened between them. "Well, I just wish to offer my sympathy," she said, holding out her hand.

Alice took it, holding it lightly and shook once. After which the woman retreated towards the door where Alice's daughter was putting on a brave face, as Alice could see, taking more guests sad words before they left. Beside her was Micky's girlfriend, Frannie, looking lost in the wash of people. The woman joined this small band.

"I wish," Alice began, "they'd stop saying how sorry they were."

"They mean well," Mandy said resignedly.

"Yes but it doesn't help," Alice's voice caught in her throat as she said this.

"Only time can do that as you know," Mandy consoled her younger sibling.

"Yes." Alice wiped a threatening tear from her eye before it could spill, smudging her makeup a little as she did. She quickly reached for her bag to sort the mess she was sure she had made to her mask in her moment of weakness. "Oh look at me, an old fool."

"Nonsense, you're allowed to shed a tear or two," Mandy tried to reassure.

"Well, I look a state now," Alice said, as she looked at her image in the compact mirror, she'd removed from her handbag. "It just doesn't make sense though. Why was he in the woods?" She asked as she tried to fix her make up.

Mandy hesitated for a moment. "I was wanting to speak to you about that, actually," she said quietly to be sure her sister was the only one to hear.

Alice looked at her quizzically, "How do you mean?"

"You know about what happened at that cottage to Frankie and the others back then?" The memory still stung deep within, even though the years had diminished it some.

Alice stared more intensely at Mandy, eyebrows knitting more closely together. "You can't even remember," she paused a moment, "right?"

"That's what I told everyone," Mandy looked away nervously.

"Why?" Alice said loudly, luckily from Mandy's point of view no one noticed.

"Because."

There was a second or two's silence before Alice spoke again. "So what did happen?"

Some how she dreaded the answer for she knew the legends that surrounded that hated, old dwelling. Why someone didn't burn it down years ago, she thought to herself.

"I'll meet up with you tomorrow in Kilmarnock and we can talk then," Mandy didn't really know how her sister would take the story she had to tell but she was sure that she didn't want to say anything here so close to the woods. She also didn't want to upset her sister with what she had found out about the paranormal over the years as she searched for a way to make sense of what she had seen back then.

"You haven't changed have you?" Alice began, feeling peeved, "Start something and then just leave it till later."

"I just don't think this is the place to be dragging out family business," Mandy attempted to placate. It worked for Alice's strained features relaxed and she agreed to meet up the next day but she insisted that it would be at her house. She also stated that she knew someone else that should be there but didn't say who. Mandy could tell by her look that she wouldn't take no on the last matter, so said nothing other than to agree to the terms.

"How is little Janice coping with everything?" Mandy asked, hoping to break the icy silence that had fallen on them by asking about Alice's daughter.

"Well you know how it goes. She's decided to go back to work tomorrow," Alice said, looking over to where Janice was seeing the last of the guests off. "She puts on a strong face, but I don't think she's giving herself time to come to terms with it."

"Have you tried talking to her?"

"Yes, though she just brushes me off. She always was a stubborn one though."

"She takes that from our side of the family. Remember what mum used to be like?" Mandy smiled at the memory.

"Yeah, true." Alice returned the grin.

"Hey mom, do you need a lift home?" Janice said, appearing at the table. Mandy could see the new worry lines on her face.

"Yes, if that's no trouble," Alice answered, glad that she would soon be home.

“Do you need a lift Aunt Mandy?”

“I’m fine, I can phone for a taxi,” Mandy replied.

“Are you sure? Janice wouldn’t mind dropping you off, would you?” Alice turned to her daughter.

“No, of course not.”

“I’ll be fine,” Mandy dismissed the offer politely. “And I’ll see you tomorrow,” she said to Alice. She wondered who the other person would be. At first she had supposed it would be Janice but now had no idea. She pushed it from her thinking, as she was sure to find out soon enough.

* * *

In the derelict building in the woods the banshee felt restless. She had caught a scent of something, someone familiar. She could not quite place the smell as it mixed with others on the breeze running through her woods from the direction of the old manor. It annoyed her that she couldn’t place it though she was sure she wanted to find out who or what it was. But the light of day, though cloudy and raining, still held her prisoner in the cottage.

She stroked a claw like finger across the glass of her jar playfully. She knew the torment that it caused to the trapped souls. In her twisted mind it gave her pleasure to think of it and for a second it allowed her mind to wander way from what troubled her. Back to the nights when she could roam freely and fill the air with her joyful scream that cause the blood in the veins of those that heard it to chill.

She gave a short laugh, which sound more like a screech of pain.

Chapter 3

Mandy was surprised by the changes to New Mills. A new estate had been built on the way into the village coming from Kilmarnock. Well at least it was new to her, though in fact by the style she reckoned it must have been built twenty years ago. The taxi carried her up the hill into the council estate and away from the memory of the last time she had stumbled onto the main street. Soon the cab pulled up to Mandy's destination.

The rough cast, grey with age, gave way as Mandy entered the brightly coloured interior. She was surprised to discover Micky's girlfriend was the other guest that her sister had alluded to the previous day. "I thought this was just going to be family."

"Well I thought that since Frannie is having Micky's bairn..." Alice said, waving her hand as if to dismiss further comment on it. "By the way Mandy, Frannie," she introduced them formerly, though they had briefly met at the funeral, “Frannie, Mandy.”

“What about…?”

“Janice has got her work and she is hardly ever around these days since moving to Killie, to busy with her own life,” Alice explained, not wanting to explain how she and her daughter didn’t get along. The death of Micky hadn’t helped bring them any closer. She made a gesture with her hand as if shooing the conversation away.

Mandy remembered the arguments they’d had when they were kids. It had always started with the same dismissive gesture of the hand but had always been her that had done it. Now she realized how annoying she must have been, yet she held her thoughts to herself. She eyed Frannie who in return was watching her with sternness to her gaze that told Mandy that the girl would possibly not believe a word of what she had to say.

“Tea, coffee?” Alice offered as Mandy took a seat facing the way she had entered the room.

“Coffee would be great, black one sugar.”

“You okay Frannie?”

“Yes thank you,” the younger woman replied as she rested her cup onto her lap as she watched Alice disappear into the hall, headed for the kitchen.

The only sound to break the silence was from Alice as she made the brew. Mandy sat feeling the awkwardness of the lack of conversation, which made her feel as nervous about the subject she was here to discuss as she felt the previous day, in some way more so.

Frannie on her part merely smiled, a forced smile, as she waited. As she had grown up she’d heard the odd rumour about the woman she now sat across from. She remembered the argument she had with her mother when she started going out with Micky. Her mother had said he was just like his hippy aunt. She had quickly dropped it when Frannie had asked what she meant. It was a friend that had mentioned the fact that his aunt was infamous hippy chick that had survived the slaughter at the cottage. Her friend had thought it funny, though Frannie hadn’t.

Other than that she didn’t really know much about Mandy or what had happened at the place in the woods. Other than this she had rarely heard anyone talking out right about what had taken place to her and her friends. Only in all those hushed conversations she'd imagined some weird hippy chick wasted on mad mushrooms and acid. This image was nothing like the smartly dressed lady she kept glancing at now.

"Here you go," Alice said as she returned with the coffee, "one sugar, no milk you said."

"Yes," Mandy said happily, as she took the cup and placed it on the table before her, careful to use a coaster.

Alice sat on the chair across the coffee table from Mandy with Frannie between them on the settee. There was a moments silence as the three women looked at each other, waiting for one of the others to speak.

"So you're staying at the Lodge, the other side of Killie?" Frannie found her voice to ask a question, though she was sure she sounded as awkward as her nerves told her she was.

"Yes, it's not been there long I take it by the looks," Mandy answered.

“It was put up about seven or eight years ago, I think,” Alice said, looking at Frannie for conformation that she was correct.

“Is it that long?” Frannie was surprised as she hadn’t thought that it been as long as that but then again she wasn’t really all that sure it hadn’t. Coming from New Mills she had rarely ever given Killie much thought unless planning Saturday shopping trips with her mates when she was younger or heading for a night at the movies.

“It looks expensive,” Alice said, sounding a little snooty. Though she was only basing this on the photos in the Standard when it opened.

“No it’s quite reasonable and very comfortable.” Mandy said, ignoring her sister’s cattiness.

“I stayed at one a few years ago,” Frannie paused a moment, “before I met.” She gave a half smile to hide her grief. The other two women could still see it though in her eyes, where she couldn’t conceal how she real felt.

“Did you have a good time?” Mandy asked, hoping that a good memory might help.

"No not really, it rained the whole time," she said and gave a short laugh.

"Where were you?" Alice queried.

"Oh I was holidaying with Susie Telford down in Cornwall."

"Telford, is she anything to do with Janet Telford?" Mandy screwed up her face.

"That's her mum," Alice answered for Frannie, "Yeah you were friends when you were at school before…" She broke off as she remembered Frankie.

"Before?" Frannie prodded, guessing there was some tad of gossip behind the story.

"Before Frankie Johnston," Mandy couldn't help but give a wistful smile at the memory, "Janet had a thing for him but it was me he had his eye on."

"Yeah and Janet wasn't best pleased when you two linked up," Alice gave a half laugh when she said this. She had never really liked Janet after all.

"So what happened to Frankie? Did you marry him or something?" Frannie leaned on her knees with her elbows, eager to hear the tale.

"Ah, if only..." Mandy's voice trailed off again but this time there was a sadness to it that Frannie could easily hear. Alice's eyes fell to the floor.

"So what happened?" The mother to be felt she didn't want to know the answer but couldn't prevent the question from escaping into the open. She also knew deep within that it had something to do with why they were here. She gazed at each of the two older women in turn, waiting for the answer.

"That is hard to say because I didn't actually see," Mandy finally said, "what I did see has been in my nightmares ever since."

"What?" Frannie was confused now.

"Mandy was one of the hippies from the sixties," Alice explained, as simply as she could, "You know that died in the cottage. Well she of course didn't, you know but..."

"Yes I've heard about that but that was just..." Frannie didn't want to say anything further.

"Well the stories about the cottage being haunted are true," Mandy said sternly.

Frannie glanced at Mandy then back to Alice and back again, mouth hanging in shock. If a fly had wanted to make a home there she would have been unable to stop it. Her mind was filled with a heavy blankness that pressed behind her eyes forcing tears to well up. Her hand involuntary came up to cover her fly trap.

"I wasn't a hippy," Mandy tried to lighten the mood, "well not much of one."

"Yes you were," Alice countered. She looked at Frannie and seeing her close to tears was reminded of their recent loss. She felt her rising anger slide away.

Mandy had followed her sister's gaze. Her head bowed as she was reminded of why she had come. Guilt pressed down on her. "Well regardless of what you thought I was, it doesn't change what I saw that night," Mandy said quietly, as she reached for her coffee.

"Okay so what did you see? What did happen then?" Alice asked.

"Well," Mandy began, "Frankie and me had met the others in the Lion. We'd spent the day tidying the cottage and making it more homely.

You know how it is when you move into a new place?”

“Yeah,” Frannie agreed. Alice nodded her knowledge of the hassle moving was.

“Well I only had a shandy though the others had a few beers before we headed back to the cottage,” she paused to take a sip of coffee. “We didn’t stay up late and I’ll admit to smoking a reefer. But it was just the one between us.”

“Are you sure it was just the one?” Alice asked not wanting to let her sister away with the admission so easily, sure that the drugs would explain whatever Mandy thought she saw.

“Of course I am,” Mandy kept herself calm. “Anyways me and Frankie had other things on our minds than smoking some dope, if you know what I mean.” She smiled at the memory.

“I bet you did,” Alice said, her mood lightening up for a moment. They all gave a laugh at this.

“Well I was young, what can I say?” Her face took on a more sombre look as she remembered waking that night. She shivered at the thought but forced herself to continue, “I woke. I don’t know why but the attic room me and Frankie shared was ice cold. I swear I could see my breath freeze as breathed out, it was that cold. Frankie was still sound to the world but I sat up. As I did something began to grow at the bottom of the bed. I sat routed to the bed as I watched it take shape.” She found she had to pause and shakily managed to take a swallow of her coffee wishing that there was something stronger in it to steady herself.

The others looked at her, afraid to ask. There faces did the asking for them without the need for words. Though Alice wanted to hear she didn’t at the same time. She felt that it sound too much like something made up to grab attention.

“Somehow I knew I had to get away and the things scream sent me flying. I knew only I had to get away. I felt myself smashing through the window and I knew I was cut but it didn’t matter I just had to get away. Somehow I made it to the village where I was found next day.”

“So what was it you saw?” Frannie asked after a moment’s hesitation.

“It’s hard to describe but it looked like a melted, disfigured person or thing. The scream it gave out of that gapping mouth and those white staring eyes.” Mandy shivered. “It was ghastly and had to get away. If only…”

Alice waited to hear more, suddenly sensing something. “If only…what?” She prodded when Mandy didn’t go on.

“Well when we were cleaning up the house I found one of those crosses we’d found all over the house. It was just before Frankie and me left to meet the others at the pub. It was in the basement and of course I took it down. Well I think that was what let this thing loose.”

How could she be telling us some horror story at a time when we have lost someone dear to us? Yes Mickey had his faults but we loved him. Yet at the same time there are the old tales of how you don’t go into the woods at night. But that is just something to scare the kids with, isn’t it? Were the thoughts that filled the others heads as Mandy finished speaking but they held their thoughts to themselves.

“I know what you think but I can assure you I had one small glass of shandy nothing more that night, nothing more. And yeah I was asleep before I saw the thing but it wasn’t a bad dream, I know what I saw was real,” Mandy could tell they were finding it very hard to take in what she had told them.

“So you’re telling us that somehow you let this thing out? Like in some cheap horror movie or something?” Frannie asked incredulously.

“Yes I think so,” Mandy felt the guilt renewed. She had thought she had gotten over it, especially after all this time but being here under these circumstances brought it back like it was fresh, new.

“Well it would make a good campfire tale,” Alice chuckled.

“But it’s all true,” Mandy wasn’t sure if she could convince them, yet felt she had too, “How else did Frankie just die and what about Mickey?”

Her words stung at the other women for a moment before Alice stung back with her own words, “You disappear for years and now you come here telling us some rubbish you made up in some drugged up haze and want us to believe you. What do you take us for?"

Mandy sat stunned, unable to speak. She hadn't thought beyond telling Alice about what had happened to her, hoping that she would believe her somehow. At the same time she had hoped that maybe she would get help to end the nightmare that haunted her dreams and the cottage. To bring to an end what she had let loose all those years ago.

"So why tell us?" It was Frannie who broke the silence that had ensued from Alice's angry outburst.

"I hoped for help to get rid of the thing," Mandy said mildly, almost in a whisper, unintentionally.

"Oh so you want us to go ghost hunting now," Alice's venom still simmered in her words, yet her eyes were wide in astonishment.

Frannie couldn't help herself from giving a giggle at the thought. She could just about see it in her mind. A pregnant woman and two pensioners in jumpsuits, jumping out of an old ambulance ready to capture the spook.

"It's not so much ghost hunting if you know where the thing is," Mandy suddenly found herself getting a little angered at having to defend herself, "and I don't think it's a ghost as such…"

"So if it isn't a ghost what then?" Frannie asked.

"I'm not sure but I have done some research over the years," Mandy had found a lot of lore on the subject of the supernatural. At first it hadn't been easy to find but over more recent years the internet had aided her immeasurably. Though she had ran away at first, the nightmares that plagued her had in some way led to find out more about what the thing she had released.

"What sort of research?" Alice asked sarcastically, "watching Most Haunted?"

Mandy looked at her sister for a moment before replying. "If I remember you used to be really into this sort of thing when you were younger," she retorted.

"When I was a kid maybe," Alice said, as her face began to colour. She glanced over to Frannie hoping for her to back her up and saw she was squirming a little at the family argument. She felt embarrassed, she hadn't meant to start arguing even if what her sister had to say was far fetched. She also knew that her sister wouldn't lie, not about something like this and at a time like this but she was an easy target for her sadness. Even if they hadn't been close for much of the time Mandy had been away, she knew deep down she was very much the woman she had been, just older and more tempered by time as well as life's losses. "I'm sorry."

"No it's me that should be sorry, maybe I should go."

"No, no," Alice didn't want Mandy to go. She wasn't sure she wanted to hear what she might be planning but she didn't want her to go. She had so looked forward to seeing her again, of remembering the happy times.

"So if it isn't a ghost what then?" Frannie had been dying to hear what Mandy thought it could be.

Mandy hesitated till Alice asked her to go on. "Well with what I've found it could be a wraith or banshee."

“A banshee?” Frannie asked incredulously, “Aren’t they some sort of lost spirit that cries out when death is near or something like that?”

“In the Irish tales they are but there are other tales where they are the bringers of death,” Mandy explained. She looked at Alice expecting her to say how mad she was being but she sat as if resigned to it now.

“So how do you get rid of it?” Frannie asked, though she didn’t really believe in it all she was ready to give some payback just to make her feel better. She had been keeping it all locked away trying to just get on from day to day, and the idea of striking out at something seemed very tempting.

“Well, usually there’s something that ties these things to a place. I think that it may be that cottage is the link.”

“So what do you want to do?” Alice mumbled, just loud enough to be heard, “Burn it down or something.”

“Why not?” Mandy demanded, happy that it was her sister that had said the words.

“What? You’ve lost it,” Alice scoffed.

"It's not like anyone is going to get hurt or even shed a tear for that old place, are they?" Mandy thought it a reasonable thing to do, after all it could end the evil that inhabited the house and free her from the nightmares, she hoped.

"Two old women and Frannie pregnant," Alice said, shocked at the thought.

"We could though," Frannie answered.

Alice looked at her with surprise.

* * *

The banshee pushed her way through the house to the attic so she could catch the sent on the wind. It was the same as the one the day before and she now knew it as it brought back the memory of the one that had escaped her wrath. As she took the girls lover, she had escaped by jumping through the glass of the attic window. She had let her go but now she had another chance to bring the defiler of her home the justice she deserved.

Tonight, she thought, tonight the hunt. She savoured the feeling of hate that welled within her bitter soul. She looked out at the track in front of her dwelling. The yellow tape that the uniformed people had put up around the garden fluttered in the breeze, now tattered. “You thought you got away,” she said softly to herself, “but you could not stay away and so I shall find you and have you yet.”

Chapter 4

"So you still not caught that ghost yet," Andrews smirked at Munroe.

"Not yet but I'll give you a shout if I need you with butterfly net," Munroe said, it brought laughter from the other CID officers that stood around Andrews, including Johnson, Munroe's usual partner.

Though Johnson could have been the one to suffer the jokes since the interview with Ferris but he had been drawn away on one of their other cases when Munroe had been duped by uniform. But he had never heard of the man before so how was he to know that he was a ghost buster freak. Munroe was sure uniform must have been in the other room watch through the one way mirror.

Though uniform had claimed later that they only knew him as a local history buff, which Munroe didn't doubt from all the dates and names the man used in his tale of who the ghost belonged to.

"Munroe!" the chief cried, from his office. Munroe turned away from the happy crowd and entered the chief's sanctum, closing the door as he did.

"So you had to go to the funeral," the chief said as if disappointed at this. An overweight man who was only to glad to have an office job, rarely needing to go out on ops and when he did it was always a back seat. Watching as his team did the hard work, backed by uniform.

"I was just showing my respects," Munroe defended.

The chief sighed. "And now you can drop it, right?"

"Yes," Munroe said. Inside though he wished he could keep the case open as he was sure that there had to be more to what had transpired.

"Sit down," said the DSI as he took his own seat behind the desk. "I know how it feels to be left with things not all tied up in a bow. We all do but you have to forget about this one, there's no evidence that anything other then a tragic accident happened at the cottage."

Munroe looked like he was about to say something but thought better of it so nodded his agreement.

"Good, now maybe you can get back down to some real work. How's the investigation into the recent break-ins up the valley coming?"

"I'm pretty sure that it's the same gang but you know how the villagers are, they want us to stop the culprits but won't give us anything that might help. Though we did get a blood sample from the one last night but now need to wait to see if it will lead anywhere."

"Good, keep me informed when the results come back. What have the householders had to say?"

"Not much,"

"Mmm," the chief nodded. "Okay. Just remember though to stop searching for ghosts, right. I know about the history of the place but it's just a fairy tale the locals made up to scare their kids with at night."

Munroe felt uneasy at the chief repeating the warning to drop his case. But he had nothing so knew he had to. Maybe if he hadn't been so heavy handed when talking to the families, maybe then he would have been able to look into it without the DSI taking an interest. He had been sure though that they must have known someone that had it in for the lads and that was why they had been running through the woods. What other explanation could their have been. So it was a given then that either the families knew something or the friends. But then they had complained about his line of questioning and the DSI had received a phone call from upstairs. Well he did have other cases to deal which offered a happier outcome.

"Well you better get back to it." The DSI dismissed Munroe.

Munroe rose and left the office with a felling of despondency. He had already decided to drop the matter even though there was something to the case the rankled at him. Yet there was no witnesses, no evidence, nothing at all to show there was a crime to be investigated. So why did he still have the gut feeling that there was? He pushed his thoughts aside as he settled himself at his desk to look over the file on the recent burglaries in the Irvine valley. His eyes looked absently at the open folder.

“That about you vanishing off to that funeral?” Johnson said, coming up behind him.

“Yeah, but its fine,” Munroe said, looking up.

“Excuse me sir.” A young fresh faced uniformed officer interrupted them. “The desk sergeant asked me to find someone to interview a suspect.”

“Suspected of what?” Munroe queried.

“An assault, sir.”

“OK.” He was glad of the distraction. “Lead the way then. You coming then?” Munroe nudged his partner as he got up.

“As long as he’s not going to blame it on the spirits,” Johnson smirked.

“Now you’re starting?” Munroe grinned playfully back.

Susie McLean stared at the screen, her eyes feeling the strain from the hour and a half looking through the reels of micro film. She wished that someone had taken the time to transfer all this old material to the computer system. Of course that would have meant spending money, which was usually in short supply for a small newspaper and even shorter supply for the local library, which was where Susie had to go to find the back catalogue for the Standard. Unfortunately it was all kept on microfilm, though plans had been in the pipeline for years to transfer it to digital format but there never was any money spare for the project. Of course Susie wondered why the library needed it as she saw enough staff apparently doing nothing when she arrived.

She rubbed at her eyes, then rotated her head to free the tension before looking at the screen again. It had taken so long because the reels weren't properly catalogued or marked for that matter. Again she thought how lazy the staff were. So it had taken most of her time working through each film till she finally found the one that covered most of the sixties. That had been just under half an hour ago. Unfortunately it didn't cover enough of the decade, stopping at December 1967. She controlled the frustration.

Luckily the next had been what she needed but now she had the main story before her she was wondering why. What was the point of searching so hard? She pushed the doubts out of her mind and concentrated on the headline staring back at her. Girl Found Bleeding In Street. Not very catchy, she thought.

She had almost not bothered looking up the old story but her curiosity had gotten the better of her. Her father told her she took it from her mother. She remembered how it had always annoyed her dad how her mum would jump to the window at the slightest excuse. She smiled at hearing the scene play out in her head, as it had so often before her.

"There should be a law against being so nosey," her father would say.

"Well there isn't, so just you mind the telly," she would answer, which he would do with a humph.

She hadn't spoken to her parents in over a month and she felt slightly guilty for not taking the time to call. She made a mental note to do so, but knew she would probably forget. Anyway, she thought to herself, mum will call in a day or so, just to give me an earful for not calling her.

She turned to concentrate on the old story. The police had followed the trail of blood from the girl to the cottage in the woods. The reporter had mentioned that locals believed it was haunted. At the cottage three bodies had been discovered though at the time police had withheld the names.

She groaned as she thought about the idea of search more issues for the names of the three. She knew though that she wouldn't be able to get any rest until she had gotten all she could from the old reports. She looked around her wishing there was at least a coffee machine close by but knew she wouldn't taste the sweet bitterness till she had finished, so concentrated on what was before her.

Chapter 5

The sun was almost set by the time the taxi arrived to take Mandy back to the Lodge. As she got into the back of the taxi she heard the screech of a fox or so she thought from the woods but it still made her jump a little. She chided herself for her foolishness but memories of the past had been stirred by the visit to gain her sister's help and talking of the past. She was glad to find an ally in Frannie who had seemed eager on the idea of burning the cottage down. She knew it sounded daft, yet what else could they do, go to the police, and tell them what she knew? And she knew how they would treat her, like some sort of nutter. No she had no choice, she had to end the horror that lived in that cottage.

The taxi turned off of the hill and headed towards Killie. Slowly she relaxed into the seat, happy that at least she and her sister had dropped the matter after Alice had said she would have no part of the stupidity. After that they had started talking about all the changes that had happened over the last forty years as well as who was married to who. Mandy had found herself laughing out loud often at the thought of how some of her old acquaintances had paired off. She wasn't surprised to hear most had split after the kids arrived, but one or two were still together. Others had left, as she had, or maybe not exactly as she had, though still they had headed for another life as she had in a way.

* * *

The banshee had been unable to hold her exultant cry from escaping. Soon the sun was down and she began to head in the direction that she could sense the scent of her adversary came from. She knew that she would need to be patient, but at the same time she wanted to rush to where she was sure the woman would be. The dark was her ally, yet she still needed stealth for she would need to enter the village. Gliding with glee between the trees avoiding the track so she could go unnoticed if someone happened along the path. This was not the night to scare foolish strangers taking a stroll in the woods.

She had no fear of the people the village, or anyone, for they could not harm her. Still she did not wish to warn her intended victim of her coming. So she planned to wait just inside of the wood, and use the back gardens of the near houses to learn the exact location from where the breeze carried the allure that drew her.

As the boundary to the village grew closer she drifted into the branches with their adornment of budding leaves, which welcomed the shorter nights. From this vantage point she would be able to identify her exact destination, as she had done in a time when she first sought out judgement against the guilty. Oh, she remembered with glee those early days, and like then she followed the boundary so as to fix the place, like an old fashioned radio operator trying to find the source of an illegal transmission.

Once she was certain of where she would go, she settled herself in the high branches to wait till the village began to slumber for the night. She glared at the bright street lighting with distrust. She watched as the strange metal boxes carried people to and fro through the streets. Whilst pedestrians, with collars up headed home to the evening meal.

* * *

Alice ritually washed her cup and set it on the draining board, before emptying the basin. For a moment the lights flickered. Not for the first time she wished she had a strip light or at least anything other than the standard council dangling light. She looked at the aging units and wondered if the local authorities would ever get round to updating the houses up here in the valley, but doubted it.

As she dried her hands, content at now being ready for her bed. She turned on hearing an out of place sound coming from the back garden. It unnerved her, fearing the house breakers that the gossip spoke of. She tried to see out of the window but it was too dark for her eyes to see beyond the glare reflected on the glass, and her reflection staring back at her. Yet she stood for a short spell before a yawn made her consider her book waiting by her bed to help bring relaxation after a busy day.

As she headed up the creaky old stairs she stopped on thinking she heard a noise from her livingroom. She stood for a moment using the banister to support her as she leaned over and listened. Nothing came from below. She chided herself for the foolishness, for she knew she was alone, and that she would have heard if someone had broken in.

Got me worrying all this talk of ghosts, and burglaries, she thought to herself. A load of, “Nonsense,” she half thought and half muttered to no one, and carried on towards the top. The lights flickered again as she reached the landing. Oh great a blackout all I need. How’s an old lady meant to read in the dark. But the lights steadied to their usual brightness, clicking them off before she cross the hall to her bedroom door.

* * *

The banshee had watched from the garden until the old woman had headed for bed. She had found it hard to hold herself from rushing in. She was angry for she knew that her quarry was gone, but she was sure the old woman would know something. And one soul was as good as nothing at all. She would surely be guilty of something, after all she was old and no one got through life as a saint. She smiled at the thought, though if someone had seen her they would have thought she was grimacing.

Once the kitchen light was extinguished the banshee drifted to the other back window, the one to the livingroom. She wanted to see what scent remained of the one she had come for. It was also too soon to confront the woman that she had watched from the backyard.

Inside she glanced around, as she inhaled deeply, savouring the scent of her enemy, though it was almost completely masked by the measly morsel's house she was in. She tapped a long talon against a glass cabinet full of trinkets, and ornaments, pictures of family, and memories of a happy life. She wondered at the pictures. So life like these painting, she thought as she stared at them, she must be as wealthy as a laird.

Her eyes locked on one old black and white in a silver frame. The picture showed two young women, the older of which was the one she remembered, the one she had hoped to find this night. But she also knew that she would have changed from this youthful figure into an aged version with the passing of the years. She studied the picture a moment longer, as the night she had escaped the banshee's clutches replayed in her mind.

* * *

Alice plumped up her pillows behind her to support her as she read. As she reached for her book the room became chilled. She shivered, and rubbed her goose bumped bare arms. Her mother's cross she had worn since the fearful woman had depart this plane rested coldly against the revealed flesh, left uncovered by the V of her white cotton nightdress.

The bedroom door handle shook as if a hand had brushed against it. At the sound Alice's head snapping round to face it. She felt twinge of pain from the sudden movement.

Unconsciously her breath was held from escaping as normal, eyes narrowed, mind frozen as she waited just for a moment. Then she carefully swung her legs free of the covers, yet kept her gaze locked on the source of her fear. Absently a hand rubbed at the dulling pain.

"Is someone there?" She challenged the perceived danger as she picked up her mobile phone from the bedside cabinet. The lamp jostled as her unguided hand rose, fingers trying to switch the device on without looking down to guide them. "I'm calling the police."

As she uttered the words the handle visibly turned releasing the door from its frame. It smoothly entered the room. The empty opening accused her of hysteria of an old mind. But for the turning of the handle she would have been sure that that was all it was. She slowly made her way around her bed toward it.

At the opening she peeked nervously around the corner into the darkened hall, the light from her lamp barely reach into it, expecting to confront the thief. Relief washed over her as she saw it was clear, sighing, and at the same time feeling a little foolish. My old peepers must be playing tricks, she thought to herself as her hand grasped the door and began to close it again. At the same time she turned. She froze to the spot, eyes glued to the figure stand looking at her intently from the other side of her bed. A smile of cruel intent played across the girls face causing Alice's heart to skip a fearful beat.

"How?" Her mind stumbled to comprehend the situation before reverting to the defence. "What are you doing in my house?" She demanded of the stranger though she couldn't prevent her legs from trembling, her words offering small comfort, or reassurance to her shaking appendages.

The banshee studied the woman, comparing the image she had from the photo. Yes, she thought, you know the one I want. She felt a tinge of disappointment as the Alice's cross winked at her but didn't show it, for she could feel the fear emanating into the room.

The phone came to life. Alice glanced down hopeful of rescue, but the hope vanished as the no signal message glared back at her. She fumbled helplessly at the buttons. It always got a signal, her mind screamed frustratingly at her.

A chuckle filled the space, playfully icy. The hairs rose on the nape of Alice's neck. "What do you want?" She asked, her eye stuck to the changing figure before her. Flesh seemed to melt, eyes turn from living to deathly white. Alice stopped her breath without thought. Her eyes widened as her throat constricted. Her mind retreated from the image and her legs the ability to hold her up. She fainted, falling half out the room. The pain would only be felt from the heavy fall when she came too again.

The banshee watched with revulsion. "A little too much for you," she said, sadly to the prostrate form. She wanted to question her, but how if she was so overcome with the fear. She decided to wait, she had plenty of time after all.

Alice moaned at the throb her arm gave as she slow regained her senses. She was unsure at first, as her eye fluttered open, how, or why she was on the floor.

"Ah, the sleeping ugly is awake," the banshee goaded.

Alice remembered the vision with a shudder. Her gaze fell on the figure of the young girl, the disfigurements gone. Alice struggled to a sitting position, her body protesting at the fall it had endured. She shook her head trying to clear it of the confusion of thoughts that babbled all at once, like a crowded room.

"Did you like the little nap?" The words were said with a tinge of sarcasm that could not be missed.

"Uh," was the only response Alice could find to muster, as she watched the creature toying with the things she had on her dressing table. "Who, w-wh-what are you?" She finally managed to ask it, shakily.

The banshee regarded her with curiosity. How to explain? She thought before answering. "Ah, that is a question. I think of myself as an angel that brings punishment to those that a deserving." She gave a chilly chuckle at her answer.

Alice gave her a distrustful look.

"What else could I be?" asked the banshee on seeing the face Alice had pulled. She was unable to hide the slight welling of anger from her voice.

“I could think of a few things. My sister…”

“Sister?”

“What?” Alice hadn’t thought that maybe it was her sister this thing wanted until that moment. Things were sliding into place in her head. Yet it was hard for her to take it all in at once, even with the creature Mandy had spoken of before her.

“And where is your sister now?”

Alice hesitated on seeing a malicious glint in the girl’s eye. “Gone,” she finally said.

“What a pity, I so wished that I could have made her acquaintance again. It has been such a time since I last met her,” the venom was clear in the way the words struck Alice. “Where has she gone?” The last question was almost innocent in the way it slipped out.

Alice paused before replying, “Away,” another pause, “back to where she came from.”

“And she didn’t even drop by to say hello to me,” the words sprang bitterly. One more scare before I leave then, she thought. At that she began her change into her horrifying beauty, letting loose her scream to freeze the soul of all who heard it. Outside dogs joined in chorus, wishing to add their voice to the horrifying song.

Alice's eyes widened in abject terror, her mind drawing itself into darkness to be free of the sound that filled the house and froze her soul. She lay slumped against the door frame till banging at her front door roused her back to the land of the living. She quickly looked for the apparition, and felt a sense of relief that it was gone.

She forced herself up using the frame of the door as an aid. Someone called her name urgently through her letterbox, it sound like her neighbour Robert. "I'm coming! I'm coming," She cried out to bring an end to the racket he was making, and began to lumber down the stairway. Soon she had unfastened the front door from it locks, opening it only wide enough to see her neighbour.

"Are you okay? Me and Jilly heard an awful scream, we thought something bad had happened," he asked, worry etched on his podgy features.

"I'm fine, just an old woman tripping over her own feet," she answered unconvincingly, "I'm fine." She gave him a wavering smile.

"Are you sure? Maybe we should get you checked out."

"No, no I'm fine really," Alice said, just wanting him to go. Yet at the same time she wished she had someone to stay with her in case the thing came back.

He looked at her warily for a second. "Okay but still you should get yourself to the doctors in the morning just to be sure."

"Well maybe, but I'm really okay," she said, giving him another grin which seemed to work.

"We're just next door then if you need us," he said and turned to head for his comfy chair in front of the telly. Though he knew his wife would nag him for not insisting on getting Alice checked out. What could he do though if she didn't want any help?

She closed her door as he reached the gate, and rested her back against it. Did I just have a fall, and some bad dream? She asked herself inwardly, but she knew she hadn't. The fear she felt was too real, too fresh for her to really put it down to that. Her gaze wandered up the stairs, half expecting the evil to be waiting for her. A sigh of relief escaped from her lips when she saw it was clear.

It was several minutes though before she found the strength to head back to her room. She retrieved her mobile phone from the floor as she entered. She felt like ringing her sister, or Frannie, but decided it was too late. She climbed into bed, putting her book aside not in the mood to read anymore. When finally she snapped off the light she lay with her eyes open staring at the darkened ceiling. A restless uncomfortable sleep, that only came in short burst, was all she managed to find for most of the night until before dawn her mind lost the struggle, and she fell into a deep well of nothingness for too few hours.

Chapter 6

Alice got up later than normal, which made the start of the day out of sorts. She still felt fatigued from the fitful sleep she had managed. The rain added to her dark mood that the tiredness seem to cause, the greyness gripping her mind in a fog. She watched the rain crashing against her kitchen window in waves. The winds howl a reminder of the unexpected visitor. The thought forced a shiver and she turned away from the window to glance around the lonely kitchen.

She made her way into the livingroom carrying her cup of tea with her. Slowly she decided that maybe she should phone her sister, or Frannie to see when they were meeting up. She hadn't taken much notice the day before for she hadn't intended to go. Now though, after what she had seen she was sure that something needed done. She also knew that there was little hope of the Ghostbusters, or such like doing it for them. She just wasn't sure that becoming an arsonist was the right thing. She didn't have any better ideas though.

How do you deal with ghosts? She questioned herself. Maybe I should have watched more of that programme Most Haunted, or something. But she had never really been one to watch those kinds of thing.

She pulled her mobile from her dressing gown pocket and noticed she hadn't turned it off the previous night. The battery warned her it was low. Now where did I put the charger, she thought. She left her mug on the table, while she quickly retrieved the item from down the side of her chair. She stiffly managed to get her phone on charge, leaving it to do its business, not wishing to use it whilst it was on charge, fearing that it may pose a danger.

She sat back in her chair, leaving her tea before her on the table. She rested her eyes for a moment, but soon drifted off. Her head slumped to the side almost waking her, though the exhausting night had been too great, and sleep in to much need for her to fight it any longer. She slumbered for over an hour, and would have felt it was worth it if not for the crick in her neck. It added to the aches she still felt from fainting like a scared little girl, as she thought of it.

She absented-mindedly lifted the cup of tea, and took a swallow. “Ugh.” She made a face and glared at the tea as if to accuse it of the crime of not staying warm.

Brrrp-brrrp-brrrp her phone announced someone wishing to have a word with her. She gave a startle jerk at it, almost dropping her cup. Luckily the tea remained held in its container, she set it back on the table.

“Hello,” Alice said, answering the impatient buzzing contraption after unplugging it.

“Alice, you sound a bit gruff still. I suppose this is a wasted call, but I just thought I’d see if you had changed your mind about today.” It was Frannie.

“No, no I was just going to ring Mandy when you rang. Yes, I would like to be there. I, I, I. Oh god.” It was as if it suddenly hit her, until that moment she had been under a cloud. With it tears threatened to leak from her eyes.

“Alice, are you alright?”

She pulled herself too as best she could before answering. “I had a bad night that is all.” She didn’t want to talk about it just yet. She knew though that she would have to at some point, probably when they met up later.

“Are you sure, I could come over if you want,” Frannie voice was full of concern.

Alice didn’t know, her mind split. She so wished for company, at the same time she didn’t want to trouble the girl as she would have her own things to be getting on with. “I’m sure you’ve got things to do, I’ll be fine,” She finally said.

“It’s no problem. I’ll be round in about ten minutes and I won’t hear another word about it, okay. I’ll see you in ten then.” At that she hung up so Alice couldn’t argue.

Alice shook her head as a smile played softly across her lips. Oh, well I better get the kettle on, and I could do with a fresh one as well, she thought before picking up her cup. And then I’ll get some clothes on, oh god I still haven’t done the house work, she thought looking around at the perceived mess her house proud mind told her was very visible to the discerning eye.

Mandy was running a little early and was expecting a wait at the coffee shop on Bank St. in Killie. She was surprised as she entered for not just Frannie was there, but so was her sister. She wondered if maybe Alice had come to try, and talk them out of the plan.

"Alice," she said, as she approached the table in the small cave like interior of the coffee shop, "I didn't think I'd see you here."

"Well can't I have a change of heart," she didn't sound convincing to Mandy, though she still felt a little taken aback by the statement.

"She had a visitor last night that made her see things a little differently," Frannie added, hiding her own doubts to the reality of this. Though she trusted that Alice wouldn't make something like this up, she was uncertain if it hadn't been just a vividly bad dream.

Mandy looked at them both intrigued by their looks as well as words. "Who?" She asked, as she unwrapped herself from her coat and took a seat facing the two women.

"An old friend, no acquaintance," Alice began, "that's not right either. Well anyways the thing you were talking about yesterday happened by last night."

"What?" Mandy's mouth hung open in shock. "Why?"

"She thinks it was looking for you," Frannie answered for Alice.

Mandy stared at the waitress as she approached the table where they were seated. "Hello, we have a special on our New York cheese and bacon bagels," the cheerful voice of the young, slender girl said.

"Cappuccino will be fine," Mandy answered.

"Another small pot of tea for us two," Alice added.

The girl scribbled the order down. "Are those orders one or should I make them separate?"

"I'll pay for them," Mandy stated before Alice had a chance to offer to cover the bill.

"Anything else?"

"Not for me. Do either one of you want something else?" Mandy offered.

"I'm fine." Frannie shook her head.

“No, thanks. Watching my figure,” Alice jested to try and lift the gloom she felt still surrounded her.

“So what happened?” Mandy asked when the waitress was out of earshot.

“I was just going to bed,” Alice began to tell Mandy what she had already been unable to stop herself telling Frannie, when she came around to her place earlier. She only briefly stopped once their beverages arrived. The waitress left the bill on a saucer next to Mandy. Frannie gave the waitress an identical saucer with the bill for the pot of tea that had been already consumed. The girl took the payment with her pasted-on smile still showing, when passing a couple of minutes latter to clear another table.

Frannie helped when Alice found it hard to continue. She would repeat part of the story that she had already heard until Alice found her voice again. When it was told Mandy was lost for words. She had always feared that the entity would still be looking for her, yet had suppressed the idea as best she could. Eventually it was, but a small hidden thing deep in her worst nightmares. Now she was felt it rise within. As it did her conviction grew stronger that they would have to act to bring an end to this.

"Aren't you going to say anything?" Alice said her voice still shaky.

"I'm sorry," Mandy replied, casting her eyes down at the table and her near finished coffee. Guilt threatened to rise within, as the evil had not been after Alice, and Mandy knew she had brought the visitation to her sister's house.

"It's not your fault," Alice told her, "You didn't know that it would turn up looking for you. Did you?"

Mandy for a moment thought it an accusation, but on looking at her sister she could see it wasn't. "No, but I did fear for a long time after my…" She for a moment found the words stuck from coming, "That it was still after me. Maybe it was the bad dreams, I don't know for sure. I never thought it would…"

"Of course you didn't," Frannie said, "but it does prove you were right." She said it even though she herself wasn't sure if this was real, or not. All she cared for was some pay back for her child who would grow up fatherless because of that old cottage, and so she was happy to go along with it for now. At the same time doubts were starting to grow at the back of her mind.

"Maybe we should get out of here," Alice said, looking around the coffee shop. As they had talked it had slowly grown more crowded than when they had placed their order. She felt as if someone near by may hear them as they discussed what was needing done.

"Yeah, we can do a bit of window shopping as we talk," Mandy suggested.

They left without further discussion only resuming as they head for the town cross, along the narrow back street. Slowly as the day worn on, and they perused the charity shops, which seemed to be in greater numbers these days than other shops, they formed a plan. Alice would provide the fuel for the required Molotov cocktail, as she had fuel for her petrol lawnmower stored in her hut. One being decided to be more than enough to do the job, as they knew it would take the fire service from Galston a while to get there.

The only real problem had been when they should do it. Alice wanted it done with, as did Mandy so she could get an end to it. Frannie strangely was the one who wished to wait for a few days. Her reason was that she wanted to see it for herself, she didn't want left out, but she had work. She needed the money now she was going to be a lone parent, so felt the need to get back to work, and not ask for more time off. She was sure if she asked she would get more time, but she had already said she would be back for the weekend shift at the shop she worked in.

Both the sisters had said that she could just take another day off. That her employer wouldn't mind given that fact that she had just lost her man. Still Frannie hesitated, unsure. In reality she was beginning to doubt that this was the right course to take. Still the need to blame it all on anything other than as some had said when they thought she wouldn't hear, just one of those terrible things that happened. And with it she strongly felt the wish for vengeance, to lash out at anything, something. So she didn't understand why she wavered, she just did.

In the end though, it was agreed to wait till Monday, three days away. Frannie would work her weekend shift at the Co-op, whilst the sisters would spend sometime shopping and catching up on old times.

Chapter 7

Munroe looked at Susie McLean with narrowed eyes. “We aren’t looking for anyone in connection with the incident, as you well know.” He didn’t like speaking with reporters, let alone this one. She was just too bubbly looking, which could make a lesser officer blab some unintentional information. If she wasn’t a reporter he might have asked her for a date, but she was. Also he was still getting over a divorce from a bad marriage, having wed at too early an age. Six months on he still felt unready to start looking for another serious relationship.

“What are the findings then? Was it the ghost?” She asked. She had joined the queue just after he’d entered the bake shop as if she had been waiting.

He gave a short chuckle. “Ghost?” He knew where she was headed with this. Another attempt at causing him more grief from his

DSI. To get a follow up on her last story, The Ghost Of Lyndon Strikes Again.

"Are you saying you haven't heard about the legend of the house where the young men were found?" She felt the beginning of her story growing in her head, "I am surprised, after all didn't you see my story on it?"

"Legend? Don't you mean something to scare the kids with?"

"So you have, but I take it you're a sceptic?"

"I work for the police, not the bloody Ghost Hunters," he answered looking at her wishing she would go away, or his order would arrive so he could.

"Can you say if you are going to interview Mickey's great aunt?"

"And why would I do that?"

"You mean you don't know?" She felt a thrill at knowing something that Munroe didn't, so she felt like savouring the moment.

Munroe waited for her to continue. When she didn't he found he had to ask, knowing she was drawing pleasure from it. "Know what?"

"His great aunt was the only survivor in the incident in 1968." She was glad to see the flicker of shock that crossed his face.

"I don't think that something that happened back then could have anything with the tragic incident that happened recently, do you?" How did I miss that one? He thought, while hoping he was hiding it from showing. Well not much I can do now I've been ordered to drop it. And really what could she tell me that I don't already know, unless she got her memory back. He wondered for a moment on that thought.

"She's staying at the Lodge." She liked the feeling of having information that he hadn't known, and informing him of it. "I was thinking of going to see her if you wanted to tag along." She knew the added weight of CID might get her something that would other wise be kept from her, like Mandy's room number, though she was sure she would get it somehow.

"Sorry I have more pressing matters," he said, his order finally arriving allowing him the chance to escape. "Well I hope you get the story," he said this with an insincere smile. He so wished he could, but knew that he would need a better reason than his own curiosity to go questioning Mandy Sinclair as she was known back then. He guessed that she would be known by a different name now, yet didn't query Susie for the name, not wishing to encourage her further than need be.

As he head back to the office he wondered about Mandy. Would she remember anything now from that night? Her amnesia may have lifted since then, maybe she could say what happened, but then again maybe she wouldn't want to. After all didn't they say that the mind protects itself through that kind of thing? But what could be so bad that you would want to forget it? Or maybe she just said that she couldn't remember because she was afraid of the consequences.

After there had been a suggestion that drugs may have been involved, and if there had, she may still think that she could face charges. She might not know that it was too long ago unless it contributed to the demise of her friends directly. His mind continued to play these thoughts over as he crossed St. Marnock Street towards the station.

He had hoped that going for lunch would lift the tension left by the paperwork he'd been snowed in by all morning. He now looked forward to the chance to head of to the last match of the season tomorrow. For this week to be over and for his life to fall back into the usual rhythm it had before two fools went stumbling through the woods at night. At least as normal as it was after his split from the years of arguments.

Chapter 8

Over the next day Alice and Mandy met up in Killie, where they would go for tea and then do a bit more of window shopping. Conversation carefully avoided any mention of Monday's business. Small talk filled part of the day and the rest seem to take care of its self. They felt closer than they could ever remember, as if the shared experience of meeting the banshee had created a bond stronger than mere sisters could share.

As kids they always acted spitefully towards one another, as some sisters know how to do best. Though they did love one another, it was never shown, at least not often enough to remember. Now those few memories came back like jewels that radiated light, and brightened the eyes of children.

Sunday came, and went. The morning of the plan arrived. Mandy rose early, earlier than her usual seven in the morning. She had breakfast as soon as the restaurant was open, but found she wasn't really that hungry, nerves playing their part. Toying with the sausage, and eggs she ordered for nearly an hour. Eventually she drank her coffee, left the rest, then retreated back to her room to get herself freshened up. Her taxi was ordered for nine as they had agreed to meet in Galston cross around half past, and she hoped to be a little early.

As she sat in the room doubts emerged out of the darkness of her mind. No matter how she tried to put them to one side they pushed back. Can I? What if I see it? Will it work? The questions drew time out as the TV presenters droned on. The news played over and over ever half hour it seemed, telling her nothing new. The presenters' interviewing the famous about their latest film, which they were starring in. Though she seemed to be watching, her attention was turned inward. She only emerged from time to time so as to gauge the time from the bottom of the screen.

As nine approached she pulled her head from the dark clouds. Her resolve began to return now that she was closer to leaving, though nerves still stirred a tingle in her chest, a tinge of trepidation was driven back as she closed the door as she left her suite, she knew that she had to carry it through. If she didn't turn up she was sure that the others would bottle out as well, leaving the evil to find more victims.

At the same time Mandy felt sure that Frannie wouldn't be there. She didn't know why she thought this, maybe it was the time she had spent with Alice without the younger woman being there. She knew this was probably unfair to Frannie, but could not stop herself from doubting the girl.

By quarter past nine she was exiting the taxi in Galston across from the Parish church, standing high above street level. The old thick high wall of the church yard created a little plaza and a house had been built in times past to share it as a gable end. She was glad to see the butchers was still where it had been since she was a kid, coming here for a Saturday shop with her mum, and sister. The memory of those happy, youthful days brought a smile to her face, and a yearning for those simpler days. She crossed the road to the plaza to wait, using the bus shelter to find an uncomfortable seat.

She didn't have to wait long, for a bus drew up as she was contemplating wither to cross over to look in a clothes boutique offering some fabulous looking ball gowns, though she had little use for such fancies. She was taken aback when Frannie got off first followed closely by Alice.

"I hope you haven't been waiting long?" Alice said, more as a statement than an actual question.

"No, five minutes at most," Mandy reassured them.

"Good, good," Alice said, "so are we ready?"

"Well as ready as I'm ever going to be," Mandy answered, a wavering smile the only sign of her nerves.

"Are you sure that this is the right thing?" Frannie had planned not to come, but then thought she may be able to talk the two women out of it. Now she was here she didn't have a clue how to, and felt like maybe she had to go along until she found the right moment to voice her thoughts more clearly than she thought she could muster now.

"Well let's get a move on then," Alice said, seeming to not hear Frannie, and began to cross to the small back street, followed by the others.

"Did you remember the package?" Mandy asked.

"No, of course I did," Alice said, tapping her oversized handbag, whilst rolling her eyes at her sister. She had also thought of the wick, and had an old dusting rag for the purpose. The glass check was in a plastic bag its lid firmly screwed down until the bottle was needed. She had been nervous on the bus as she thought she could smell it but no one else seemed to notice, not even Frannie, who had to reassure Alice that it was fine.

Alice had sensed that Frannie was unsure of what was planned as they travelled together on the bus, but had been too concerned about her package to ask her about it. Now as they walked she was ready to talk. Find out if the young woman was still alright with what they were about to do.

"Are you alright Frannie?" Alice was unsure how else to broach the subject.

"I've just been thinking over the weekend, you know," she answered hesitantly.

The banshee stroked her jar, listening to the pleas from the imprisoned souls. Only she could hear them but it mattered nothing to her that she didn't have anyone to share her pleasure. For she was happy enough with the thoughts of the fear she brought to the few she revealed herself to.

The night before she had enjoyed the fun of chasing a drunk home. He had been so sure of himself when he first came across her crouching in an alley. "Hey young chick-a-dee, looking for a bit a fun?" He slurred at her, as he wobbled uncertainly on his feet.

"That depends on the fun," she said, as she rose to face him in all her glory. His face had dropped like a stone. The embrace of the alcohol had vanished, replaced by sober fear.

He had stumbled backward before turning to flee as quickly as his overweight frame would allow. She had cried only half of her frightening scream before pursuing him. She had quickly tired of the chase, knowing that he would run till he found refuge in the hands of the disbelieving.

That was fine. She had her enjoyment after all. A diversion from the usual haunting of the woods that surrounded her dwelling. She cursed herself for not leaving the woods for so long. The first time in a century or more had been to the woman's sister's home a few days ago. She had needed the diversion after the disappointment of that evening. She had hoped for more yet achieved little. Her enemies escape had reminded her of another who had evaded her wrath.

She drifted up to the ground floor into her darkened kitchen. New boards block the daylight out, allowing her the freedom to roam from her dungeon. The attic only had the one window which faced away from the sun's brightness so was always a place she had spent the latter part of the day. Over time it had become a favoured place to watch the trackway that ran to New Mills.

The dark was no problem to her eyes. With death had come the ability to see into the darkest places. A gift she hardly noticed now, but at first found so wonderful, for it aided her in her hunts. For the revenge she had sought.

She moved down the hall toward the blocked aperture that once served as a front doorway. As she did voices drifted through the thin, cheap plywood. The old rotted door lay on the floor, discarded by the workmen sent to secure the old house. One caught here ear, in a flash she saw the image of the old woman in her mind. The one from a few nights before, when she hoped to catch another.

She floated up to the attic to see who she was with and where they may be headed.

* * *

Alice unwrapped the plastic shopping bag carefully. Once free she removed the rag she had brought for a wick. Mandy and Frannie glanced down every so often as they kept watch in case someone happened along the path towards the theme park, or coming from it. It was unlikely though at this early hour as the park didn't open for a couple of hours yet.

"You'll need to soak the rag in petrol," Frannie commented. She had been unsuccessful in her attempt to dissuade the others, though she hadn't made a good argument. Part of her still wish some payback, and now she was here that feeling grew.

"And it looks a bit much, so you better tear it down a bit," Mandy added.

"Yes, yes, any more pearls of wisdom while I'm down here," Alice answered testily, as she unscrewed the cap on the glass soft drinks bottle.

"I was wondering about how we're going to do this?" Frannie said, taking a good look at the intended target.

"Well, I thought we just throw the lit bomb and there you go," Mandy said, as she looked over at the building and noticed what Frannie meant.

Alice glanced also, and studied the problem. "Could one of us put it through that top window?"

"I don't know if I've got it in me these days." Mandy said, suddenly thinking that Frannie might have been right when she said that it was a mad scheme, as the walked up from Galston.

"I could do it," Frannie said, to the surprise of the others as well as herself. She had hoped that she would find a way to talk the others out of this. She had told herself that morning that this was her only reason for coming. Now stood before the place where the father to her coming baby had died, she felt a renewal of the grief and with it the need to strike out. Even if it was this meaningless act of destruction.

"Are you sure?" Alice asked, stopping what she was doing for a moment to look at Frannie.

"Well, yes," Frannie said, "that's why we're here, after all."

"It's good you came," Mandy said, "or we may have had a bit of a problem."

Alice finished making the Molotov, and stiffly stood up. "Well here you go. Are you sure you can do it?" She repeated her question just to be sure that the younger woman was okay with the task at hand.

"Yeah, no problem," Frannie assured Alice, with a nervous smile as she took the petrol bomb. "Has one of you got a light?" The words felt strange, as if asking for light for a smoke, something she had given up when she found out she was with child. It seemed like an age, and a half had passed since then. Yet in truth she was just beginning to show signs of carrying a new life, but only if you looked closely.

“Oh yes, the matches,” Alice stooped to retrieve her bag from the ground at her feet. Rummaging inside she soon found the small box she usually kept for lighting her gas cooker when the electric ignition failed, though it seldom did. She handed them to Frannie then realised she wouldn’t be able to do it her self.

Her first attempt at putting a match to the wick failed as she moved the stick towards the cloth, barely moving before fluttering out. The others looked at her impatiently as she tried again. This time she cupped her hands around the flame to protect it, and moved more cautiously, just as she remembered doing in more youthful years when share a light for a cigarette with friends. The wick caught quicker then any of them thought it would. They stared at it for a moment as if hypnotized.

It was Mandy who managed to pull her thoughts to the task that was still to be done. “Well are you going to just hold it?”

“Eh, no.” Frannie moved closer to the derelict building. Holding the bottle low near the base, she swung her arm back then smoothly forward trying not to let the bomb spin head over heals. It all went to plan until it dipped at the last moment and clipped the lip of the windowsill. The glass shattered, yet with some large sighs the women watch as the fuel, bursting into flame, leapt in through the gaping hole. Though some had dribbled down the front wall, most had exploded in through the broken window.

The flames seemed at first to die away. The women feared that it wouldn’t catch, that their plans were flawed. Just as disappointment began to rear its head crackling flames began to rise as the wattle in the walls, and ceiling acted like tinder. Breaths were released in unison as a satisfying sigh.

“Thank God,” Frannie expressed her relief, “I thought it wa…”

A chilling, soul churning scream rose from the house. The women stared at its source, but could only see the licking flames at the window frame as they grew stronger. The colour ran from their faces at the sound of the unearthly screech.

As it died away Frannie thought for a moment she saw something moving within the growing fire. But it was so brief she would have dismissed it if it hadn't been for the awful sound. "Did you see that?" She asked once the only sound was the growing blaze.

"What?"

"No, what did you see?" Mandy asked shakily, the sound having brought back dark memories of the last time she had heard that scream.

"I don't know, just a shadow I think," Frannie said, as much to convince herself that it was nothing. The doubt still lingering till she voiced it, "Was there someone in there do you think?" Panic waited, ready to seize her.

"No," Mandy said, "Not living anyway." The certainty of Mandy's voice relieving Frannie's fears.

"Do you think that was it?" Alice asked, still staring at the fire. "That sound? Did we get it?"

"We better get moving," Mandy ignore the questions for now as she noticed the smoke growing in density as more of the interior caught.

"Maybe we should," Alice agreed.

The older women began heading towards New Mills. Frannie stood a moment longer, her gaze searching the flames. When she pulled her attention away she strolled quickly after the others.

* * *

The banshee's anger raged within. How dare they? She thought, that lying crow, she said her sister had left, was gone. How dare she? If only she didn't have the protection of the cross I would show her.

She had felt a tinge of fear when she had risen into the attic to see the growing blaze. Then rush to try it put it out, but had caught the sight of the three women who had caused it, standing staring up at their handy work. She had screamed her anger before realising the danger that the fire represented to her precious jar.

She made her way back to the basement cell behind the hidden door. Panic and fear consuming her as the flames ate away at the roof beams. There she had waited for the flames that never came though she could hear the blaze above in the main house. Then the strangers came as the air filled with a strange whining sound. The fire was soon being extinguished as she crouched, guarding her key to bring revenge.

Hours past and the day grew late, but still the voices came from above. At one point they even descended into the basement. She had waited, ready to spring to the defence of her home. But they left without discovering her. All the time she waited, anger grew from the despair .of the destruction she knew had descend upon her home.

As night came the voices left. She waited to be sure they were gone before surveying the wreckage. Only the small kitchen and basement had survived untouched. The roof beams had pulled down part of the front wall. It was a shatter shell that remained. The sight fuelled the resentment within, the hatred.

"You will pay," she said, the words dipped in the vinegar of odium.

Chapter 9

“It was bound to happen,” the burly fire chief said to Munroe.

“I’m only surprised it hasn’t happen before now,” he answered, gazing at the ruins in the dying light. The fire was out, but it had done a fair bit of damage to the dwelling first. Amongst the smell of burned wood still lingered the taste of the accelerant.

“Probably kids,” the fire chief added, turned and headed towards his car, “Hopefully we’ll get something from that glass fragment that I gave you, and catch the little sods before they decide to torch something else.”

Munroe nodded as he followed, after one last glance at the shell of the house, wanting to get back to the office to make a report as well as book in the evidence. He wished to get it out of the way, and put this to bed before someone tried creating links to the history of the place. Though he knew that it was of little interest to anyone, after all it was just an empty derelict building in the middle of nowhere, but people loved to talk, which could lead to who knows what.

"I'll send you my report once I write it up," the fire chief said as he got in to his vehicle. He didn't wait around for further discussion. No sooner strapped into his car he, and he was driving off towards Lyndon Castle.

Munroe sat for a few minutes resting his head back, trying to clear his head. Just as Munroe pushed the key into the ignition of his transport, a flash new looking car drew up in front of his. He looked balefully at the driver. Susie smiled happily at him, glad to have caught him before he had left. Munroe lowered his window as she approached his car.

"I was hoping I'd see one our best here to investigate," Susie said sarcastically.

"Not much to investigate as you put it," Munroe answered quickly, hoping to make this short, "just kids entertaining themselves no doubt."

"So you have no reason to think that it may be connected to other recent events?" She hoped that he may slip, and give her something, anything would do for a by-line.

"I can't see how you can link the tragedy that cost the lives of two young men to this." He worded his answer carefully knowing Susie would twist is words if he didn't.

"I would have thought that it being the same location would mean it could be a possible," she tried to trap him.

"Well at the moment our belief is that it was some local kids," he countered. "That is unless you can give me more to go on than your suspicions."

"What suspicions would they be?" She tried to confuse the issue.

"I'm sure you would know better then me," he wasn't going to let her catch him out, "Anyway I need to be going so if you could move your car into the side so I can get past." He nodded his head to indicate she was blocking his escape on the narrow dirt way.

"Oh am I blocking you in," she said with a sly smile, "well I suppose there's nothing here for me then. I'll just back up, and get going too."

She slowly walked back towards her car. She reached in, and pulled a camera from the interior, and then fiddled with it for a moment, or two. Munroe tooted his horn impatiently. She took no notice, instead she moved closer to the shell that remained of the cottage. The flash indicated her snapping shots, once, twice, three times, and Munroe sounded his frustration again. Even though he knew she was doing this on purpose he could not help himself from getting annoyed at her.

Finally she seemed satisfied enough to leave. Still she teased, backing up her vehicle slowly. Munroe followed cursing under his breathe. At last they reach the theme park, and he had room to overtake, and speed away before she could turn, not wanting to give her a chance to block him further.

As he left Susie behind he had a nagging feeling that she might know something he didn't. Though he hadn't been paying attention to her, he had noticed the smile she had given him. Maybe just a ploy, after all, he thought, she did try stalling me.

* * *

Her anger drove here to impatience. She sailed over the rooftops till she was able to descend into Alice's back garden. She was just in time to see her quarry about to leave. The banshee was able to control her rage, and so sail into the air onto the roof. A horseless carriage advertising its services waited for the passenger.

Once it set off carrying Mandy away, the banshee followed high above. Like a hot, fiery breeze she followed the metal beast taking her foe down the valley toward the big town. Tonight, she thought, you will not escape my justice. She travelled farther than she had ever done in life, or since, but no fear could cloud her mind. She was too consumed by her desire to bring the true terror of her judgement upon this destroyer of homes.

* * *

As Mandy entered the lobby, the door she had just gone through rattled as a gust of wind blew it open momentarily again. She glanced back at it before turning back to the main desk to retrieve her room key. She felt happier than she could remember. A weight that had sat heavily on her most of her life was gone. With it she had a lightness to her step as she headed for her suite.

As she shut the world out, she dropped her key on the small chest of drawers against one wall. Her earlier elation had dwindled somewhat, and now she was feeling a growing emptiness. She had felt like a young girl earlier. Now her age seemed to press on her as familiar aches reminded her she was no longer that energetic youth.

She hung her coat over a chair. Letting her bag slide to the floor and looked around her lonely room. Another early night, she thought to herself as her eyes fell on her latest bedtime book. It was not her usual fair, and she was finding a hard, boring read. Yet it did put her to sleep well, by forcing her into a state of mind numbing ennui. War and Peace would have been an easier tale to digest, she thought.

* * *

The banshee took form in the empty room she had seen the woman enter. A moment of panic at the thought that her prey had somehow escaped filled her. A sound came from a closed door. She waited happy in the knowledge the noise told her, that the woman was still there.

The door opened and the woman stopped at seeing the figure standing in her room. "Who are you?"

"Ah, don't you recognise me? I thought that you would at least know whose house you burned down."

Slowly fear crossed Mandy's face. "But how? You should be…" Her words tailed off, unable to grasp how she had failed to lay the creature to rest.

"Ha-ha, you thought you, and your friends could destroy me so easily," the banshee mocked her foe.

Mandy look towards the entrance to the suite, and began to edge towards it, keeping her back to the wall. Fear made her legs feel as if they were ready to give way, ready to betray her to the floor. A sudden anger welled up within her pushing the dread aside. "What right do you have? You killed my friends. You took my nephew's life. How dare you?" She shouted at the creature.

"How dare they, and how dare you? Come to my home uninvited, and now you've burn it down." Hatred burned in each word causing Mandy to shrink before the banshee. "I was innocent, and they took my life, and what for? My home. Now you would try the same? You people think you can just take what you want. Who do you think you are?"

Mandy had managed to get near enough to the door. Now she took her chance, and rushed forward the last few feet. As she gripped the handle the banshee let her anger out in the scream that Mandy had heard so often in her nightmares. As the door swung slowly open, she tried to squeeze herself through the widening opening her legs finally lost the power to support her. She fell out into the hall.

Other guests watched in growing horror as the banshee wasted no time. No you don't, not this time, the banshee thought. She had taken on her terrible visage of melted flesh. Her scream rose in chilling intensity as she thrust her taloned hand into Mandy's back, reaching in, and grasping the vessel of her soul and tearing her life force from its receptacle. Mandy's lifeless form sprawled at the creature's feet.

Footsteps retreated quickly as the banshee cried out in exultation. Finally she had her revenge against this woman, and she wished all to know they could not escape. Her scream echoed along the emptying hallway. Then she rose into the air leaving the dead woman, taking her soul to the prison where she held all her captives, in her jar.

Chapter 10

Frannie sat down on the sofa and placed her dinner on the coffee table next to the mug of tea. Dinner was a strange statement for the sandwich, but it was all she could bring herself to make, and even this now seemed too much. She stared at it for a moment then un-muted the TV just as the adverts came to an end.

As the titles of the next program began she felt a draft coming from the open living room door, she rose to close it. Standing in the doorway a pale girl stood staring at her with cold impassionate eyes.

"What the…" Frannie began, "Who the hell are you?" Anger rising from within. How dare she just walk in here? She thought to herself at the same time.

"Don't you know?" A question answered her. "I thought you saw me when you visited my house?"

“I don’t even know you so could you please leave?” Frannie said, placing her hands on her hips.

“So why did you come to my house?”

“I don’t know what you’re talking about.”

“Oh so it wasn’t you setting fires today, it was just someone that looked like you,” the banshee said demurely, yet somehow it held a sarcastic coldness to it.

For a moment Frannie was taken aback. How could this girl know about that? She thought. Guilt grew, and with it she began to wonder if she had been seen. “How did you know about that?”

“I saw you from my window,” said the girl, her eyes narrowing.

Frannie’s arms crossed over her little bump protectively, as it began to dawn on her who, or what was facing her. “But you can’t…”

“Ha-ha-ha.”

The laughter cut at Frannie’s nerves as fear began to seize hold. Words became caught in a knot on her tongue that held them from finding a release. Her mouth hung open uselessly.

“What? Has the cat got the brave girl’s tongue?” Mocking words slapped at Frannie, “Not so brave on your own, are you? Ha-ha-ha.” The banshee was relishing the moment. She enjoyed the trembling that began in Frannie’s legs as she transformed before the woman, terrifying her even more. The banshee’s only hope was that the woman wouldn’t pass out like the other, with fright.

Frannie stared with wide eyes at the ghastly creature that now stood before her, blocking her only escape route. Her legs refused to do anything more useful than shake. Her mouth worked soundlessly, like a fish gasping for breath. As the scream filled the room a whimpered sob echoed feebly back at the thing. It advanced on her, yet her legs refused to move her back. Then ice seized her heart, and her legs folded under her. Her eyes stared at the arm that had thrust into her chest. Strangely she wondered why there was no blood as darkness descended upon her.

The banshee removed her hand as if she had been jolted by electricity. She stared in surprise at the girl shocked by what she had felt. Two souls, she was certain, but how? Two souls intertwined in the one person. Then it dawned on her, she was pregnant. It was the only explanation, and anger burned at being thwarted in her act of vengeance.

"You are with child," the banshee stated, with a tinge of anger seeping into the words, to the coughing, spluttering woman.

Frannie's left arm was filled with pins as she tried to drag some air into her lungs. The darkness at the corners of her vision cleared painfully slowly, with a protesting throb in her head. She sprawled on the floor staring up at the fearful sight of the creature. It seemed even more frightening gazing up at it, more menacing, more dangerous.

"I would have your soul," it screeched angrily at her, "but for the innocent inside you." The banshee glared at her with a burning hatred that Frannie could almost taste.

"What do you want?" Frannie managed to force the question out as her breathing came a little easier. It all seem somehow unreal to her, and she found that her mind filled with clouds that prevented her for taking everything in.

"You will find out in time," the banshee said, then leaned in closer as if to renew her attack, "I will punish you yet."

The smell of the things so close was over powering bring bile to rise from the depths of Frannie's stomach. She rolled to the side trying hard to control the wrenching of her whole body as it came up. The effort caused more darkness too fill her vision for a moment. Pain burned in her chest, and she found herself short of breath, as her left arm tingled as if it were asleep. She took her time gathering her strength.

As she turned back to where the creature had been she was relieved to find herself alone, but the shaking from the terror she had endured continued. She began to search for the mobile before realising that it was still in her jacket.

Frannie was struck with dizziness on trying to gain her feet forcing her to sit next to the pool of rancid bile. She could feel that she needed help, but was unsure if she could get to her phone. The knowledge that she had to warn Alice forced her to drag herself to her jacket. She speed dialled her number, as she slumped to the floor again. Feeling as if she would be unable to herself from sliding into sleep, she put the phone to her ear.

"Frannie?" The familiar voice came through the earpiece.

"Alice, it was here," she managed to get out before the darkness consuming her.

"Frannie, Frannie," came the desperate voice of Alice, but Frannie could no longer answer.

Chapter 11

"Detective Munroe!"

He turned to see Susie waving a notepad in the air as if he hadn't heard her shout. He let out a sigh. He should have guessed she would be here, was the thought that ran through his mind. He glanced around the lobby of the Lodge, wishing he could avoid her.

Munroe had been the unlucky last to leave CID and so had just been caught when the strange report of an unusual death at the Lodge arrived. Therefore it had been up to him to investigate, now he wished he had left the office five minutes earlier. Or even wrapped up his questioning of the few witnesses to come forward, not that they had seemed eager to answer his questions.

"So I understand that it was Mrs. Mandy Brown who has died?" She asked as he approached her.

"Yes," he replied rather flatly.

"You know she was Micky's aunt?"

"And I suppose you believe there is a link?" He asked mockingly.

"Well it is strange, don't you think?" She countered.

"In which way?" He continued the cat, and mouse questioning.

"Well she was the same woman who survived the deaths back in sixty eight, and then her nephew, and now she seems to have died in strange circumstances, wouldn't you say?"

"This isn't the cottage. In fact that is some eight, or ten miles from here. So I can't see how you can link what happened here to her nephew's death, can you?"

"Well I'm not so sure? After all there was also the fire today."

Munroe didn't want to go down this speculative road at the moment. It had been enough of a shock when he had recognised the deceased when he arrived on the scene, from the funeral the previous week. "You can't really think that this woman had anything to do with that can you?" He thought it very unlikely that a woman of Mrs. Brown's age could possible be setting fires to abandoned old houses in the middle of nowhere.

"Well that would be for you to find out I would have thought."

"Unless you have some information I don't, I can't really see how there is any connection. Do you have something that you wish to share?"

"No just doing my job, and trying to keep our finest on their toes," Susie said with a smile that suggested to Munroe that she did, and just wasn't in the sharing mood at the moment.

"Well if you don't have anything then I have reports to work on, and the family to inform," he said, trying to escape.

"And I suppose there wouldn't be a chance that I might join you?" She asked, but knew this was never likely.

"I'm sorry, but you know, procedure," he was only to glad of that old excuse. At that he left to find his car in the parking lot. Susie watched him go before following to find her own. She didn't wish to let him off the hook so easily.

Munroe phoned the station to confirm the address as he drove towards New Mills. With his destination confirmed he headed straight for Mandy's sisters house. He dreaded this side of the job, and knew he could have left it to uniform to do the deed of breaking the terrible news, but felt a duty to do it himself. After all he had been the investigating officer after the woman's nephew had been found dead. He knew the family, even if they hadn't been on great terms, he felt it would come easier from someone they were acquainted with.

As he travelled the twenty minutes, or so to Alice's house, he began to wonder if there could be a connection to the fire that day. Yet he failed to understand how, so why did the reporter seem to think there was? It was a coincidence, but his policeman's instinct told him there was no such thing. It only ever appeared there was, though in truth it was because there was usually a connection of some sort.

He found Alice's house with ease. Disappointment washed over him when he didn't get an answer. He knocked again in his most forceful of law enforcement knuckle bruisers. Still the house remained silent. A neighbour appeared from next door as he was just about to turn, and leave.

"She's not in," the large set woman said.

"Do you know where she may be found?"

"I'm not sure," she began as if mulling something over, "if you want I could take a message, or you could leave a number, and I'll see Alice gets it."

"No, I need to see her myself," Munroe knew that the woman was just looking for some local gossip to fill her life, "I'll call back."

A car pulled up behind his, and Susie alighted from it. Munroe felt he should have known she would be headed here. He turned back to the woman at the neighbouring doorway. "Actually I really could do with speaking to her," he said as he withdrew his warrant card, and showed the woman.

"Oh, you're with the police," the woman acted surprised, "well I suppose I can tell you. She is a way to the hospital with Frannie, her grandson's partner. She had a bit of a turn and Alice went over to her house, and had to get an ambulance. Such a shame after what happened to Micky, you know."

"I see, thank you," he said quickly wanting to get going before the woman kept him standing there talking for the next hour.

"Detective, surprised to see you so soon," Susie said sarcastically as she arrived at his shoulder.

"Yes I'm sure," he replied coldly, "And what does the Standard want here?" He made sure the neighbour knew what this new arrival was.

"Just doing my job, you know how it is," Susie said, giving him a cold smile.

"Mmm, yeah," he said to her, then turned back to the neighbour, "Thanks again," he said to the neighbour, and headed to his car.

Another twenty minutes later he was at the Crosshouse hospital. At the desk he showed his warrant card so he could get the information to where Alice maybe found without any questions. Finding an elevator he headed up to the wards. His only hope was that the woman he was here to find would have already left. Yet he doubted this, life was seldom that simple. If she was already gone he planned to leave the bad news to uniform to sort out in the morning.

The ward was broken into small rooms off the main corridor with six beds to each. Frannie had been put in one of these half way down the long passageway. Alice was sitting by her bed looking worriedly at the younger woman, who was look very pale.

Alice looked up as he approached. As recognition dawned on her, her brow crease, and she frowned at him. "Detective…" She struggled to remember his name. Her face was lined with worry for her friend.

"Munroe," he offered.

"What brings you here?" Alice asked, as Frannie lay back against her pillows.

"Could we talk somewhere more private?"

"Private? Is something wrong?" She regarded him curiously. She wondered if he knew something about what she and the others had been up to that day. If he was there to arrest her, but she quickly dismissed the notion, telling herself that he wouldn't have wanted to speak to her privately.

"If we could just speak somewhere a little less…"

"We can speak in front of Frannie, I trust her," Alice cut him off.

"It concerns your sister Mrs. Mandy Brown," he said solemnly.

"My sister? Is something wrong??" She asked worriedly. Fear rose deep in her stomach. Her mind began to race with thoughts of what had already happened to Frannie, and she wondered if it was possible that the evil had somehow reached out to her sister too. After all she hadn't answered her phone when Alice had tried to phone her earlier to tell about Frannie.

"If we could just speak somewhere quieter," he tried again.

"It's okay." Frannie patted Alice's hand to reassure her.

"I'll be back soon," she said to Frannie, forcing a smile.

Munroe noticed she too had the same fearful look that Alice held on her face. He dismissed it, believing it was simply down to the younger woman's medical condition. He hoped it was nothing serious as the family had had to deal with too much over the past month, or two.

With the use of his police ID he was able to get one of the nurses to show him to an office behind the nurses' station. He ushered Alice into a seat, taking another from behind a desk and sat close to the older woman. Dread was now beginning to be driven away as he now focussed on relay the sad tidings.

"I'm sorry to have to inform you that tonight I was called to the Lodge just down the road from here," he began unsteadily, trying to find the easy way where there was none, "It is my sad duty to tell you that your sister was found deceased at the hotel."

Alice slumped, her mouth hung loosely as she stared in stunned shock. Her mind reeled into its self as she took in the news. "It was it, wasn't it," her mouth seemed to say of its own accord, "the banshee."

He looked at her stunned. What did she mean? The what? Banshee? "I don't understand. You do know what I just told you?" Was she having some sort of breakdown, he wondered.

"Yes," she said sadly, "how did it happen?" She seemed to focus on him.

"We are still to determine that at the moment, but we will know more once we run tests," he answered, not wishing to say autopsy. Not wanting to voice his belief that it was a heart attack.

She looked down at her hands, wringing them. "It was the banshee, I know it was. First it went for Frannie, now my sister just like it tried before, and it came for me the other night, last week, and it will be back to finish the job, I'm sure." Alice didn't mean for it to spill out, yet couldn't stop herself.

"I don't understand. Banshee?"

"Yes, as in evil spirit!" She exclaimed.

Munroe shook his head. Evil spirits, she must have lost her mind with all the loss she had suffered, he thought. "I know this is hard for you but…"

"I know what I'm saying sounds mad, but it's true," she looked at him hoping to convince him, yet doubting she could, "If we hadn't burned down her house, or if Mandy hadn't tried to move into that house all those years ago with her boyfriend, and their friends. I don't know, maybe then that thing wouldn't have gone after her, or Frannie, or me," she said, casting her gaze back to her hands. Tears filling her eyes.

"Do you know what you just told me?" The question came automatically as he tried to digest what Alice had just revealed. "That you are admitting that you committed arson."

"Yes, I know, but you have to understand we thought that by destroying that house we would send that thing to where it belongs, hell," as she spoke tears leaked down her cheek.

He sat for a moment thinking of what to say. He knew he should be arresting her for setting the fire, but found he didn't want to, he didn't have the heart. She had suffered a lot recently, and she had so much more now descending upon her. But she had hinted at something, something to do with what had happened back in 1968, hadn't she. His thoughts fixed on this.

"What did you mean the first time?" He hoped his question wouldn't be met with a retreat. “Did your sister remember something from the past?”

She looked up at him, and for a moment he thought he saw her withdrawing away from telling him. Just as quickly she seemed to fold. “She told me the day after Micky’s funeral,” she began, resigning herself to telling all. “She told us that it was an evil spirit called a banshee that killed Micky. She knew it was because it was the same thing she had escaped from back in ’68. I didn’t believe her, well you wouldn’t would you, but that night it turned up at mine. I don’t know why it didn’t kill me. Maybe it was because my neighbour came to the door when it let out that awful din, the scream. Just thinking about it,” she said, giving a shiver at the memory, “Well you can imagine. Then I knew she was right. So we acted to drive it back to where it came from, but we failed, didn’t we?”

“And I take it Frannie was in on it?”

“I, I,” she suddenly realised she may have landed Frannie in trouble with herself, “I, oh god. We had no choice, what would you have done, knowing what we did?”

“Well I find it a little hard to believe that some malevolent spirit is responsible for what happen to your sister, or anyone else for that matter,” Munroe responded.

“See that’s what I mean. You find it hard to accept, I did when Mandy told me, but I saw it,” She said adamantly, “I know you must think I some sort of mad old woman, but you have to believe me.”

“I’m sorry, but I don’t,” he said bluntly, “I know by what you have told me that you do, but you do understand that it does seem a bit too far fetched. Ghosts, evil spirits they don’t really exist.” He shook his head, unable to accept what Alice was saying.

“And what did happen to those lads all those years ago, or my grandson, and what happened to my sister?”

He could see that he would never convince Alice that her idea of what had happened just couldn’t be true. “I can’t really say, but I can assure you that I will be looking into the matter. Though I suspect there will be a reasonable explanation for everything.”

“But you still don’t believe me,” she said, sorrow tinged the words. “I suppose you’ll have to arrest me now?”

“I by rights should, shouldn’t I?” He looked at her for a moment like a school teacher would a naughty child they had decided to give one more chance. “But I can’t see how it would do any good, just give me more paperwork to fill out.”

Alice sagged with relief. As she did the fact that Mandy was gone washed over her, and tears welled up in her eyes again. They left channels in her powered face. “Thank you,” she found herself saying as a strangled whisper after a moment.

“I’ll keep you informed of what the coroner’s findings are concerning your sister,” he said perfunctorily, before standing to leave, though he hovered unsure how to make the woman feel better.

“That would kind of you,” Alice said through her tears, “but I think that the banshee will be after me now, and I may not see you again, at least not in the flesh.”

He looked at her for moment, uncertain of what he had heard. At the same time a chill played up his spine giving him a creeping feeling of dread. He shook his head slightly to clear the thought of the prediction from his mind. “I’m sure you’ll be fine,” he tried to reassure her.

She gave him a half hearted smile before he left. She stood for a moment, wiped her face. Then headed back to see Frannie before visiting time came to an end. She decided it best not to say anything to Frannie about her sister. It would be better just to say that the detectives visit was about the fire, and hope this would be enough for the young girl. But Frannie already seemed to know.

Chapter 13

As she drifted up the stairs to wait, gloating at the memory of her achievement earlier. Though she had failed to take the soul of the younger woman, she had reaped that of the older one. Now she had to be content with the thought that though she could not take her sisters soul, she would at least send her to her doom. She had formed the plan she now undertook when she had found the house empty.

The elation she had felt as she placed Mandy's spirit into the jar had given her an idea. An idea of how she may bring some justice to the last of the three. If she couldn't have her soul she could at least send her to her death. And so she had travelled to her house, hoping fear would be enough to cause the desired effect. Now she had a better way to achieve what she wanted.

She was slightly disappointed when she found the house silent, though the downstairs had been well lit. She searched fruitlessly for her intended victim, but she was not there. So she waited, formulating her plan as she did. A feeling of cold pleasure filled her as she drifted to her place of ambush. A small giggle rose within as her mind as she turned over the thought. It was barely a whisper of a breeze, but it sounded too loud to her, and she forced herself to contain the fun she was having. How alive this night had made her feel. She hadn't felt so alive since she had become the banshee all those centuries ago.

Wistfully she let her mind drift back to those glory days when fear of her filled the valley, touching everyone in its grip. Then they had quivered in fear of her, but she had only been after those who had said falsehoods against her, and brought the memory of her mother into disrepute. The ones that had sent her to an early grave.

* * *

Alice was tired after her busy, tragic day. Filled with grief she just wished to get home, and was glad as the taxi drew up in front of her house. The hall lights still blazed giving the house a warm feel in the dark of the night. She quickly paid the fare, and exited the private hire.

As she closed the world out, she felt an unease. She was unsure of what it was, just something seemed out of place, yet everything appeared as it should, as she looked around downstairs. She hung up her coat in the hall then made for the kettle to get some warmth from a mug of tea. As she waited the feeling persisted. Again she pushed it aside hoping that her prediction to Munroe would be wrong. That it was only her daft idea that played on her mind.

The kettle was slow to boil, and as it finally clicked off floorboards above creaked unusually. Alice's heart missed a beat, her ears twitched as she strained to listen. No more creaking was heard. She sighed before continuing making her brew. She still couldn't quite shake the tension she felt from her shoulders.

In the living room, with her tea set on the coffee table, Alice got out of her shoes, and into her slippers. She lifted her cup before settling back in her comfy chair. With the TV remote she called up the sky menu to find something to watch. After fruitless search she flicked it to Road Wars. It often staggered her as she watched this program, how much the police had to contend with. Tonight she also felt a little guilt at the memory of her part in the arson attack on the old house, but soon forgot that as she watched a car chase through Bristol city centre. As she viewed the action, she was able to leave her own worries, putting them to the side as she got lost in glimpse of other peoples' troubles.

By the time the adverts came on she had finished her tea, and felt it was time to read her book in bed. She switched the TV to stand-by, deciding not to go pulling the plug. Tiredness stung at her eyes as she left her cup in the kitchen unwashed. She grabbed a packet of crisps from where she had them stored in the top cupboard. She felt to the stirring of her empty stomach, though didn't really feel up to more then the crisps.

With the front door made secure for the night she began to ascend the stairs. They creaked there typical complaint at her weight. The sound reassured her, glad to be surrounded by the normality of it. It had been such a day of madness, which had been almost like whirl wind carrying her along to a wearying loss. But Frannie was safe, and would be fine with the care of the doctors, and nurses, she was sure.

As she turned to switch off the top landing light a scream filled the house. She turned to its source as the light vanished, taking a step back as the banshee rushed towards her in the last blink of light. Her foot found nothing to support her. Things slowed down as she found herself cart wheeling backwards. Strangely she thought how she hadn't been able to do cart wheels since she was child. The packet of crisps raced her to the bottom.

As her shoulder then her back made contact with the stairs pain replaced all other thoughts. Still she twisted, and fell back, the pain turning to agony as muscle, then bone bruised, or broke with a sickening crack. Her heart beating rapidly and she found she couldn't suck the air into her lungs as she continued this never ending fall.

Finally Alice came to a halt, crashing into the floor at the bottom of the stairway. She managed at last to take a ragged painful breath. One shoulder rested awkwardly against the side wall. Her legs still lay half on the stairs, twisting her torso oddly. At first a numbed feeling replaced the painful, tumbling fall. All too soon the agony began to burn into her brain. She groaned in complaint, a small barely audible squeak of a sound.

She turned her head as much as she could on hearing the creaking stairs as the banshee descended to her. It crouched by her, and seemed to be smiling. Its cold regard sent shivers of fear up the back of Alice's neck causing the hairs to rise on her arms and neck. Though she tried to steady her breathing, each intake of air became harder to draw in, creating spasms of fresh agony. It was quickly consumed in the greater all over pain that cried out from every other part of her. She half hoped that what had saved her before would come to the rescue again, yet knew it was unlikely.

"Oh, you look so beaten up," the banshee said, "Not to worry death will be with you soon I'm sure." It chuckled at its own apparent wit.

"Go," Alice struggled to speak, "to… hell."

"Sadly not, but you will very soon," it said, the words dipped in poisonous ice.

"Well leave me be to have one last bit of peace." Alice had to force the air into her lungs against there protests to say it as strongly as she could. It cost her though as her next breath was so shallow she saw dots in front of her eyes, and her brain swam to stay conscious.

"I would, but I find this so much fun," the banshee said gleefully. "And just think how you will never see your sister again."

"Bitch," gasped Alice.

"And once your friend has had her baby I'll pay her another visit, and this time she will join you sister to feed me, ha-ha-ha," tormented the banshee.

"Alice!" A cry came from the door to the side of where Alice lay in the last struggles of life. Banging on the wooden entry accompanied her name. The flap of the letter box lifted and the eyes of her neighbour peered in squinting to see in the dark. On seeing the woman's legs a shoulder was used in an attempt to force entry. Curses could be heard before another try was made at the door.

Alice's eyes slowly lost there focus, and she drew a grasping last breath, releasing it with a deathly rattle. With her death the banshee left for her home. The door finally gave, and Alice's neighbour rushed to her side to find there was nothing for him to do, but await the arrival of the emergency services and keep other nosey neighbours from entering the house.

When he had heard the scream, whilst he watched the telly with his wife, he had guessed that Alice had had another fall. He hadn't expected it to be so bad.

Chapter 14

Detective Munroe saw Susie waiting at the front desk as he entered the station. He shook his head inwardly as he made for the security door, but as he was about to punch in the number to gain access, he felt a tap on his shoulder. He turned slowly hoping she was here on other business other than last nights incident at the Lodge.

“I was waiting for you,” she said sombrely, holding her excitement at the added twist to her newspaper article. “I was wondering if you or another officer was in charge of the investigation into Alice Shaw’s demise last night?”

He looked at her blankly for a moment taking in the news of the woman’s death, hoping not to show the shock it brought. “I’m sorry, but I can’t discuss that at this time,” he answered, hoping to put off any further questions till he knew what had happened. The memory of Alice’s prediction came back to him, and he began to wonder if maybe she had known something after all.

"You did know she fell down the stairs last night at home, and was found by a neighbour?"

"You seem to have the facts so what do you wish me to tell you?" He tried to give the impression that he had been informed, but wasn't certain that it sounded right.

"I was just wondering who the investigating officer was. After all you have had a lot of contact with the family, and I thought that you might be the one assigned the investigation."

"As I said, I can't make any comment at this time," he repeated with a little more force.

"Will there be any statements about this or the incident at the Lodge earlier yesterday evening, and do you think there might be a connection between the two sisters' deaths?" Susie asked, hoping she could weasel something from the CID man.

"I'm sorry, but I have a busy day ahead of me, and I can't possibly make any statements until all the facts are known." At that Munroe left Susie as he went through the security door, as the sergeant at the desk buzzed him through on seeing his dilemma. Munroe made sure to pull it closed behind him, just to be certain the reporter didn't try to follow.

As Munroe enter the main CID office the DSI came out of his glassed off room. "Munroe could I see you for a minute, and you Johnston?" He didn't wait to see if they were moving to join him as requested.

Both men entered the chief room together.

"Shut the door. This will only take a minute, but I want some privacy," the DSI said, without looking at either of them.

Munroe closed the door, wondering if he had done something wrong.

"Take a seat," the chief said, motioning to the waiting chairs. Once they were seated, the chief ignored them as he sat across from them, regarding an open file. Munroe guessed which one it was. "I was looking over your notes on what happened at the Lodge last night." He looked up at Munroe, and then drew out another file from beneath the one he had been looking over, "And also the one on Mandy Brown's sister's accident." He seemed to mull this over for a moment, whilst watching to see if Munroe knew about the second death. When he saw no reaction he continued, "I want you, and Johnson on these. I've already told Andrews, he was the attending at the New Mills scene."

"But there's no link is there?" Munroe seemed puzzled.

"And I didn't say there was, but the family will find easier if you work both, especially after recently losing another family member and they know you so it may give you kudos with them." The chief looked at the two officers as if he expected a comment. "Some of these statements from the incident at the Lodge will need looking at again. They don't make a lot of sense, which will need doing ASAP before any of the witnesses leave. By reading these from last night you would think we'd all stepped into the Twilight Zone, and we can't be having that kind of mess can we?"

"No," both Munroe, and Johnson answered together.

"Good, Munroe you will be the lead on this, but that doesn't mean you leave Johnson out like you did last case you worked together," the DSI said, unhappily at Munroe's propensity to work alone, "do you understand? You work together."

"Yes chief," Munroe said, and looked over at the smiling face of Johnson, who loved every minute of Munroe being put in his place. It wasn't that they didn't get on, or work well together, it was more that Munroe just had a tendency to forget he had a partner at times, and would rush off before realising he'd left Johnson behind. Or whoever he was working with.

"Right on you go, get it done," the DSI dismissed them, handing the files to Munroe as he got up to leave.

Outside the office Munroe opened the file on Alice. There was nothing to indicate that anything untoward was at play, but he couldn't forget her prediction at the hospital. He closed the file as he passed his desk, and left it there.

"Aren't we going to look at the files together?" Johnson asked, with a cheeky smile.

Munroe had almost forgot him, locked in his own thoughts. "The chief said we needed the statements that uniform gathered last night clearing up," he explained, "so I thought we should go get that done first. After all there isn't much in the files to talk over that I can't say on the way."

"You taking up poetry, or something?" Johnson chuckled at his own humour.

"What?" Munroe squinted at him as he followed close behind.

"Never mind," Johnson dismissed the joke. "So we're heading over to the Lodge to interview the witnesses again?"

"Yeah, and by the time we've done that we can get a free lunch with any luck from Jimmy." Munroe gave Johnson a wide knowing grin. Jimmy was one of their sometime informants, though he seldom had anything useful in the information department. Still he was always good for a free lunch, as he was also the chef at the Lodge.

"Well I always say that there's nothing wrong with a free lunch," Johnson said happily.

"You get the car, and I'll get you out front," Munroe said, "I just want to have a word with uniform. See what they know about what happened to Alice Shaw before we go, okay."

“Fine, I already heard the talk this morning when I got in.”

“I take it there wasn’t much to it, simple fall, but no harm in hearing what the sarge has to say,” he explained.

“Okay see you out front.”

Munroe watched Johnson’s back as he left.

* * *

Susie brushed her hair behind her ear as she got out of the car. After her fruitless search for information from Munroe she had decided that she needed to get some facts first hand. So she had driven out of town for New Mills to visited Alice’s neighbours. Her only hope was that they would be more forthcoming now that tragedy had struck again. She wasn’t interested in anything, but gossip.

She knew that sometimes good stories came from half truths and as much fiction. Facts were good, yet they had a habit of killing an otherwise great newspaper article. Only enough facts so you were never accused by the readers of not knowing what you were talking about was one of the things she knew drove the modern newspaper industry.

It didn't take long for her to get to where she was going. Wisely she decided to avoid the neighbour from the previous evening, and pressed the bell on the other neighbour's door. She could hear the sound of someone coming to answer just as she was about to reach for the buzzer again so forestalled pressing it again, not wishing to annoy. She smile brightly as the door opened trying to appear friendly.

"Yes, can I help you?" The woman asked.

"Hello I hope you can, I'm from the Standard, and was hoping you could tell something about what happened last night, and maybe a little background on..." she paused for effect wanting the woman to think that she could do with as much help as she could give, "Mrs. Alice Shaw?"

The woman looked at her for a moment, "You won't have to put my name in the paper will you?" She asked. "'Cause I don't want folks thinking I'm sort of busy body."

"No, after all my understanding so far is that it was just an unfortunate accident, is that correct?"

"Well you best come in," she said. As Susie past her she gazed out along the street in both directions as if checking to make sure no-one was watching her guest entering. "Would you like a cup of tea, I was just about to put the kettle on?" She asked, as she showed Susie to the living room, ushering her to take a seat on the sofa.

"That would be lovely, thank you," Susie said.

"I don't like talking about my neighbours but," she paused as if thinking it over, "well, she isn't with us now so I don't see the harm, Miss…"

"Just call me Susie."

"Well I'm Tracy," she said, then left her guest to busy herself sorting her tea when the kettle boiled. She rejoined Susie with a tray within five minutes. Biscuits adorned a plate in the centre of the crowded shining tray.

"You must be very upset with your neighbour's sudden passing," Susie said, hoping to bring Tracy around to what she was here for.

"Yes, a really nice woman," she said, "Milk, sugar?"

"Just milk please."

"A really nice woman, as I said," Tracy continued, as she settled herself in her chair while serving the tea, "she had a bit of a fall the other week. Me and my husband were just going to bed when we heard her scream. It scared the living daylights out of me, I'll say. But that time of course she was fine. My husband did say to her to go to the doctor. Of course you can't force someone to go if they don't have a mind too." She finished pouring the tea, and gave Susie her cup.

"You are so kind," Susie said, playing along with the woman putting on the airs, and graces.

"So, your husband was the one to find her last night?"

"Yes that's right dear," Tracy said, "Do you want a biscuit?" Tracy offered up the plate.

"No the tea is fine, thank you," she answered, waving a hand in front of the plate, "I'm trying to watch my figure."

"I don't think you have much to worry in that department." Tracy regarded Susie with a twinge of jealousy. "Now where was I. Oh yes, he saw her through the letterbox just lying there at the foot of the stairs. She must have taken an awful tumble. Mind she was no spring chicken." She nodded her head.

"I understand that she was related to a Mrs. Mandy Brown, is that right?" Susie hoped that pretending not to know this information would get the woman to tell her more about the family background.

"Oh you mean Mandy Sinclair as she was known when I knew her. Mind that was before that business with that cottage in the woods. They say it's haunted, but that's just a lot of nonsense if you ask me."

"So what did happen? At the cottage I mean," Susie asked, already knowing the official story.

"Oh, that was like away back in the sixties," Tracy began, "I think it was around sixty eight or there abouts, I was just a kid. Mandy began hanging around with the wrong sorts, taking drugs, and that kind of thing, you know? Oh what were there names again," Tracy paused as she sought the names in here head, “Frankie Anderson, Jim Thomson, and…. John Dunlop, that’s right.” She nodded as she remembered them. “Frankie and John had been down in England for a bit. Up to no good if you ask me, and only came back up here when it got too hot down south for them. Anyway Mandy fell in with them and somehow they got this notion to move in together, but they weren’t that flush with cash, and we all knew about the old abandoned cottage out in the woods. So they thought it would make a great place to set up house, or should I say commune, for they were all into that hippy stuff. Well we all were in our own way I suppose.” She stopped there to take a sip from her cup, and then placed it back on its mat on the coffee table, and then took a chocolate biscuit from its wrapper before taking a nibble.

“So you knew them well?”

“I wouldn’t say I knew them well. They were a little older than me, but we all knew each other back then. Ran in the same circles, friends of friends, family of friends, that sort of thing, you know.”

“Yes,” Susie smiled.

“Well when I heard about them moving into that old house I thought they were mad. After all as kids none of us would have went near the place, not even if you had paid us, of course as I said they were older, and should have known better as I saw it back then.”

“Why was that?”

“Well we all thought it was haunted, didn’t we. Childish nonsense really. Apparently some old spinster lived there once, and she was thought to be some sort of witch, or something, and it was said she haunted the house. No-one would stay there after that. As those that tried it got chased off by weird noises,” Tracy said confidentially, with a nod, “of course that was just what our parents told us to keeps us from going there. Old houses can be dangerous places after all, and us grown ups like to scare kids so they don’t go where they shouldn’t. So at some point someone made up that tale. Of course when we were kids,” she nodded knowingly, “we swallowed every word.”

“Didn’t anyone ever get curious?”

“Well there was Tommy. Oh, what was his name again?” She paused for a moment before continuing, “Anyway he, and his friends claimed they had been there, but nobody believed them. Well not till he had an accident. He got knocked down on Main Street. Of course to all us kids it had to have been because of the curse of the ghost. As I said a lot of nonsense, but we were young and pretty gullible back then,” Tracy chuckled at the memory of those bygone years.

“Aren’t we all at that age?” Susie sipped at her tea, laughing along with her host.

“I suppose we are,” answered Tracy, still chuckling. “It’s a lot different now though. Kids have got those games thingies they play, and you don’t see them on the streets much, unless they’re causing trouble that is.” Tracy nodded her head.

“So what happened to Mandy? Did she ever say what happened at the house?”

“Well she had amnesia, or so she claimed afterwards,” Tracy said, “Of course we all knew that it had to have been drugs. You don’t go jumping out a window, as she did, in the middle of the night on whim, do you?”

"But if the house was haunted," suggested Susie.

"That might explain her getting a scare, but to jump out a window in the dead of night, and there was the three dead boys she left behind. No, I can't see it myself," Tracy shook her head, "As I said, drugs the only thing that could explain it all. Of course if you wanted to know more about them you could always talk to Alan Ferris. He's a bit of a local historian, and was good friends with Frankie for a time, that was before Mandy came along, but I'm sure he could tell you more than I could."

"And where would I find him, Alan Ferris?"

"If you wait here a minute I should have his address somewhere," Tracy said, rising to get it. She headed into the hallway, and got her little book of numbers. "Ah here we are," she cried out triumphantly, returning with the book. "Now where's a bit of paper to write this down for you?" She soon found pen, and paper.

"Thank you, you're so kind," Susie said, as she received the address. "Did you know that her sister was visiting for Alice's grandson's funeral?"

"Yes I saw her coming, and going a few times over the past week, along with Frannie. She was Micky's girlfriend. She's carrying his baby, you know, poor girl left to bring the little thing into the world by herself. And then she had that turn last night, I heard."

"What turn was that?"

"I heard it was complications due to all the stress," Tracy gave a concerned frown.

"Will she be alright?"

"Well they kept her in the hospital so it must be serious, I hope it works out for her though."

"Did you hear about the fire at the cottage?" Susie enquired, ignoring the news of Frannie, but keeping a mental note to visit the hospital to see her.

"Yes, in fact I saw Alice, Frannie, and Mandy coming from the woods. I had been down at the shops getting a few things for my man's dinner, and I saw them just as I was headed up the hill. I don't think they saw me though. It was strange though for they must have saw something as I could see the smoke coming from the woods, but at the time I never thought of it," Tracy said, pondering over it for a moment before dismissing it.

Susie drank the last of her tea, thinking about what the woman had just revealed. Her mind whizzed at the idea that these three women may have had something to do with the fire. She didn't hear fully what else the woman said, just registering that she was reminiscing over her past. When Susie was sure that the woman had come to the end she set her cup down. "Well it was lovely to talk to you, but I must be getting on. No rest for the wicked and all that," she said cheerfully.

"Oh, of course," Tracy said, feeling a little at a loss, "well it was nice to have a bit of company, and if there is ever anything else you need to know, you know where I am."

"Yes, I will and thank you, you were most helpful," Susie said offering her hand. "By the way do you think that Frannie's turn last night may have had anything to do with Alice's fall?"

"Well she did go rushing over to Frannie's, and that would have put an awful strain on her, but you can never really say with these things, can you?" Tracy said, as she saw Susie to the door.

"Well thank you again," Susie said, shaking Tracy's hand a second time.

"Aw, it was good to have some company while my husband is at work. I'd get a small part time job of my own if there were any, but you know how it is these days," Tracy rattled on as if to delay Susie leaving.

"Thanks for the tea, bye."

"Bye now, and do drop back if there is anything else you want to know." Tracy reminded Susie, hopefully.

Chapter 15

"Johnson over here!" Munroe cried across the dinning hall.

The other man quickly made his way to where Munroe was seated. "That was a waste of a morning if you ask me. Why can't folks just stick to the facts, and let us get on with what we have to do?" Johnson moaned.

"I take it you got the same run-a-round as I did," Munroe said, "Oh yes, I thought I saw someone, but I can't be sure," he mocked one of the dumb things he had heard. "How could she not have seen someone in a well lit hallway? Oh I ordered your lunch for you, Steak and chips fine I hope."

"Yeah great, thanks," Johnson answered, putting the menu back down, which he had just picked up. "What I find strange is last night uniform took down what these clowns' saw, and now they deny saying anything at all. One claimed they were asleep at the time the woman was attacked, but got woken up by the screams. So I asked how he knew she was attacked, and the smart arse says why else would I be asking questions."

"Why the hell they got moved to different rooms from the ones they had last night I don't know."

"And on the other side of the complex. It's not like forensics was there all night."

"Exactly," Munroe shook his head glad to see his free lunch finally arriving, "Ah here we go, steaks up."

"Didn't they think that we would need to interview them again?" Johnson said, as his meal was placed before them.

"Enjoy your lunch," the waitress said, with a smile that looked pasted on.

"Well there wasn't anything that would tell us anything, unless you got more than I did?" Munroe queried.

"As I said before, just a lot of crap. So what now?"

"Well, not a lot on this one until we see what the coroner has to say, but my feeling is that she had some sort of stroke, or heart attack," Munroe answered, before filling his mouth.

“It wouldn’t explain her screaming like that, would it?”

“I suppose with the pain she might scream out, or in trying to get help,” Munroe said thoughtfully.

“If it was a stroke I’m not so sure she would have been able to scream, after all don’t you lose the ability to talk when you have a stroke?”

“No idea.”

They both ate in silence as the restaurant slowly filled with dinners. They both spotted one or two faces of the people they had interviewed, but ignored them. In equal measure they were paid little attention as the people were led to their tables. The sun began tentatively look in the large windows before a cloud forced it to hide again.

“So what next?” Johnson looked up from his near finished meal, feeling filled and hoping for time to rest to let the meal settle.

“Well we could make our way up the valley, and talk to the sister’s neighbours. See what they have to say about what happened there,”

Munroe suggested, equally wanting to start the afternoon slowly.

"Yeah, that sounds good to me. I could do with a slow afternoon."

"Well we'll have a brew, and then make a move, tea or coffee?"

"Coffee for me, need the caffeine."

"I know what you mean," Munroe greed, signalling the waitress as she passed their table.

"Yes can I get you something else, desert?" She asked, as if in a hurry.

"Just two coffees if you please, thanks," Munroe said, admiring her pretty young face as she wrote down their request. As she left them Munroe's phone chimed an incoming call. "Yes, Munroe," he said into it.

"DCI Munroe, Sergeant Burnett here. Uniform just arrested two youths after getting a call to a break-in in Galston. I thought you might want to know since you've been investigating the recent spate of burglaries up in the valley."

"I take it they have been taken to the Galston station for now?"

"Yes, until it's decided if they'll get police bail, or held over till morning."

"Well, I was just going up that way so I'll drop in, and interview them there, thanks for calling. Inform Galston that I should be there in about half an hour to an hour."

"No problem."

"We need to drop in at Galston on the way. Maybe a break in the burglaries up that way," Munroe told his partner, as he put his phone back in his jackets inside pocket.

"Uniform will be happy getting the collar," Johnson said.

"Yeah, well as long as we catch the buggers."

"And there was I wanting a quiet afternoon."

"At least it's on the way."

* * *

"Well that was another big waste of time," Johnson said, as he guided the car onto the main street heading back towards Kilmarnock.

"Well we didn't really think we would get anything new," Munroe said. He still felt pleased to have closed the other case earlier. The two youths had admitted to most of the house breaking over the past few months. They were now being transferred to Kilmarnock till they could go before the judge in the morning. Munroe expected that they would be bailed then.

"What do you make of the reporter?"

"Susie McLean, let her run her wild goose chase." He was amused that she was given the name of the local historian. Though he was very knowledgeable in local history, Munroe saw him as nothing more than a local fruit cake. He remembered his interview with him after the death at the cottage with disdain.

"Ferris, do you think she'll take him serious, you know, about the ghost?"

"Well, as long as it keeps her out of our hair."

"You're joking, you mean you aren't looking forward to seeing her again," Johnson said with a snigger.

"As long as you blind me first," Munroe replied, secretly though he did fancy seeing her again, but in a less formal way.

"We could always arrange that if you want," Johnson smirked, "So why would the neighbour send her there?" He asked more seriously.

"Well he is good on all the local history around these parts," Munroe informed his partner, "so I take it she wants to know about the case involving Mandy Sinclair."

"Mandy Sinclair?"

"Mrs. Brown, the woman that died at the Lodge."

"Oh," Johnson said thoughtfully, "so what did happen. Is that the old case file you had brought up from storage?"

"That's right, I thought you knew about that," Munroe said, he didn't really want to go down this road again, yet knew he would have to explain it all to Johnson now. "She was the only survivor from some goings on that happened in the old cottage where the two deaths were that I investigated. She jumped out of a window, and when officers were sent to see why they discovered three dead. One was her boyfriend, and the others friends of theirs'."

“So what happened?” Johnson ignored the reference to the other case being Munroe’s, for he had worked on it to. Unlike Munroe he hadn’t let it get under his skin.

“She claimed not to remember what transpired, and there was no cause found to the demise of the others,” Munroe said, not wishing to share any more.

“And so that would mean that she is related to one of the young men that died there last month,” Johnson surmised.

“Correct, but I can’t see how any of it has any connection, can you?” Munroe turned to face Johnson.

“It is strange though, don’t you think?” Johnson pondered, he could see why his partner had pulled up the old file now. Though when he had first done so Johnson had found it as fun as the others because of the ghostly myth that surrounded the old house. Munroe didn’t inform him he hadn’t known about the connection at that time.

“Maybe,” Munroe conceded, turning back to gaze at the car ahead. He knew that Johnson would think it even stranger if he knew about

Alice's prediction of her death. Either that or he would think Munroe had lost a marble, or two. It had been hard enough for him since he had been assigned the case looking into the deaths of Micky and Andy.

"Have you still got those old case notes?"

"No, and I wouldn't go looking for them if I were you, the DSI wouldn't like it," Munroe replied, hoping to drop it.

"I suppose your right," Johnson said after a moment.

"And you don't want to end up being the butt of the joke."

"I think I'll leave that for you," Johnson said with a Cheshire grin.

"Thanks."

"What did you think of what the neighbour said about seeing Mrs. Brown and Mrs. Shaw coming from the woods on the day of the fire?"

"I'm not that sure, I don't know we can read anything into it," Munroe tried to dismiss it.

"Still maybe we should have a word with Frannie, is it?"

“Maybe.” Munroe thought it over for a moment. “But what would we really gain, it’s not like anything valuable was lost, or anyone put in danger.”

“I suppose, but if she saw something, or was involved?”

“Can you really see two old women and a pregnant girl setting fires?” Munroe grinned at the picture in his head.

“No, but stranger things have happened. Maybe you’re right and it would be a waste of time.”

Munroe relaxed inwardly at hearing this.

Chapter 16

"If what you're saying is true, why hasn't it been investigated by physic investigators before?" Susie asked.

"Ah, that is simply because it is only known about in the local area, and you know how secretive small communities can be," Allan Ferris explained.

"But you said that it was a banshee, aren't they sort of like harmless?"

"If you listen to the Irish tales about them wailing when a member of the family is going to die, yes," Ferris began, "but here in the west coast of Scotland there have always been darker tales. Here we find vengeful spirits fill the legend of the banshee. In some cases it was even thought that they could steal souls to feed on, of course that is just a little fanciful." The idea brought a chortle of laughter from him.

"And this is what you think lives in the cottage, some sort of vengeful ghost or banshee?" Susie found it hard to hide her scepticism.

"I know it sounds mad, but when you take in the history of the place, even just the last forty years. The deaths linked to the place from the three that died in nineteen sixty eight, and then more recently two more," Ferris sounded like he was talking to a child, trying hard to convince them to eat their veg.

"And now there is Mandy and Alice that could be added to the list," she let slip.

"The Sinclair sisters?" Ferris showed his surprise as much on his face as in his voice. "How? When?"

"Last night, I'm sorry I thought you knew," she lied.

"I'm not shocked at Mandy. But Alice, what did she do to bring down the banshee?" He mused, still letting the news sink in.

"I thought you may know something," Susie egged him for any glimmer of information he might be able to offer.

"Well there was the fire yesterday. I take it you did hear about it?"

"You don't think they might have had something to do with what happened at the cottage?" She had thought this earlier when the neighbour had told her that she saw the two women and the younger one coming from the woods. She didn't want to let anyone else in on what she knew though. One loose word and with gossip, who knows who might get wind of her story.

"Well they did have a motive, don't you think?" He nodded his head conspiratorially.

"Yes, but they weren't spring chickens," Susie put forward.

"It doesn't take much to set a fire, especially where no-one is going to notice you doing it," Ferris suggested.

"But wouldn't the fire have driven off the ghost, or whatever it is?" Susie changed tacked.

"Not if the house isn't the thing that holds the spirit to this plane," he began, "it could be something that is in the house that has some significance to the ghost from her life."

"But that would have to be something old, if what you told me already about who you believe to be haunting the house," Susie thoughts rambled, "and would the fire have destroyed everything in the house?"

"Maybe and maybe not, it depends how much damage to the house there was. As for the ghost, she did stay in the house for a good part of the early nineteenth century. Of course my only other suspect was even earlier," Ferris said, in a matter of fact tone. He took a drink from his stained mug of coffee. He had offered Susie something to refresh her when she had arrived, but she had thought better of it on seeing the inside of his cluttered home and was now glad she had politely turned him down.

"Earlier?"

"Yes, well there was a girl in the late seventeenth century. She was put to death for witchcraft and afterwards there were some strange goings of, unexplained deaths that in a way was a little like what we have seen recently. Of course the records from that far back are sketchy at best," he said, leaning towards Susie as she scribbled some notes in her notepad.

"Do you know who this girl was?"

“All I have is a first name, Helen,” he answered, slightly perplexed that the reporter seemed to think differently to his theory, “As I said though she was put to death at the stake, and if you know anything of the spirit world, fire is a sure way of making sure that the spirits of the deceased don’t return from the grave. That was why it was a favoured way to dispatch those accused of witchcraft.” He glared defiantly at her.

“I see,” Susie nodded, not wanting to upset the expert. “So you say that fire is one way to banish these ghosts, why didn’t the fire at the cottage do the trick?”

“As I said before,” he said condescendingly, “the building was not the object that is holding this being in this plane of existence, and whatever it is that holding it to this world has to have survived the fire.”

“Of course, sorry for my naivety, this is all new to me,” Susie said apologetically, closing her note book, “I’m grateful to you for giving me your precious time, but I should be making a move. So much to do, you know how it is.” She gave him as warm a smile as she could muster and held out her hand, hoping that her reluctance to do so didn't show.

"It was a pleasure, and if you need to know anything more…" He left the rest unsaid as he took her hand.

"I will thank you."

She was glad when she reached her car. She gave Ferris a wave as she pulled away. She needed to go home she felt to shower. It wasn't that the house, or Ferris had been dirty, just very untidy and his cup could have done with a good wash. It was more the way he had leaned in close to her. At times he seemed to be leering with excitement over her. It was probably just the chance to talk on his favoured subject to someone, she told herself. Yet she still felt unclean from being in his presence.

As she drove, heading for home in Kilmaurs by the back roads to avoid traffic, she began to digest all he had told her of the history behind the myth of the supposed banshee. She slowly came to the decision that a better idea would have been to Google the information. Yet she knew that you couldn't find everything on the web, but decided it still didn't hurt to see if there was some site that may tell more.

She knew she still needed to find time to visit the hospital. So many things, she thought as she took her mobile from her bag. She barely slowed down as she connected it to the hands free. She had the number for the hospital saved on her phone, one of the many useful numbers she kept there for just these times when she needed them.

"Hello, Crosshouse Hospital, how may I help you?"

"Yes I was wondering if you could tell me how my sister is doing?" Susie knew this lie would work best in getting her the information she wanted.

"Of course could you give her name please?"

Chapter 17

"One of Mrs. Shaw's neighbours informed us that she saw you with Mrs. Shaw and Mrs. Brown coming from the woods yesterday. Could you tell us whether you saw anyone who was acting suspiciously?" Johnson asked.

"What?" Frannie asked, looking lost. She still could not quite take in the news that Alice had fallen down the stairs, and was dead.

"Did you see anyone acting suspiciously, hanging around the woods on your walk with the two women?" Johnson showed his impatience's.

"No, not that I can remember," Frannie answered close to tears, "I'm sorry but this has all been such a shock."

"Yes, we can understand, but we were just hoping that you might have seen something," Munroe said, hoping to cut off Johnson's inquisition. He had hoped not to have to interview Frannie, but Johnson had raised the subject again and would not be put off. In the end Munroe had decided that he had to go along with visiting the unfortunate girl.

“I’m sorry,” Frannie shook her head.

“Well thank you for giving us your time,” Munroe said bringing the interview to an end. Johnson glared at him. “And we’re sorry for your loss.” The words sounded hollow. It seemed to Munroe that he had said this once too often to the young woman.

“Thank you,” Frannie said meekly.

As the two officers left the hospital Johnson turned to Munroe, “What the hell was that. Are you trying to get off with her, or something?”

“Going in heavy like you were doing wasn’t getting us anything,” Munroe said angrily, “She told us they went for a walk, nothing wrong with that, and pressing her while she’s in hospital isn’t going to get us any brownie points, is it?”

“I just have a feeling that she knows more than she is telling.”

“About what? The fire or something else? Do you think she got up out of that hospital bed and threw her friend down the stairs?”

"Of course not, but there is more here than meets the eye, I can feel it," Johnson tried to reason.

"Feelings don't count unless you have evidence to back it up, and we don't," Munroe pointed out, "Anyway the fire isn't the crime of the century, it was only an old derelict building in the middle of nowhere."

"It's still a crime."

"Maybe, but not one anybody cares about."

"Oh-oh, here's the press," Johnson said, nudging Munroe's arm as they left the lift on the ground floor.

"Ah DCI Munroe, I take it you were here to see Frannie?" Susie asked, as she approached.

"Miss McLean, what brings you here? Hope nothing serious?" Munroe avoided the question.

"No, just visiting someone," she replied.

"Well if you'll excuse us, we have some paperwork with our name on it," Munroe said, guessing who she was there to see.

"Any news on the case at the Lodge?" She enquired hopefully.

"You know we can't say anything until we have completed our investigations," Johnson put in, wanting to get away from the reporter.

"Can you tell me if you are looking for anyone in connection to the incident then?"

"Not at this time," Munroe said firmly, "Now we do have to be going," he added bring the conversation to an end.

* * *

Susie turned into the side ward that she had been informed where Frannie was. She had checked Facebook so she would recognise her, but it took a moment to spot her. Her eyes passing over her two or three times before Frannie's face matched with Susie's memory of the face in the pictures. Though she looked thinner, and looked to have aged a lot. That could be just an old picture, she thought to herself.

"Frannie?"

"Yes?" Frannie looked questioningly at the woman who'd just approached her bed.

“Hello, my name is Susie McLean, and I was hoping to ask you a few questions concerning recent events at the old cottage in the woods near Lyndon Castle, if that’s alright?”

“I’m sorry who are you again?”

“Susie Mclean, I’m from the Standard,” she answered.

“The Standard,” Frannie said, showing her discomfort.

“Yes, I understand that your boyfriend was Micky Shaw?”

“I’m sorry, but I really don’t want to go over this all again, if you don’t mind.”

“I know this might be hard for you, but with the deaths of both Mr. Shaw’s grandmother and his great aunt, you understand?”

“No, I don’t,” Frannie lied, hoping this simple untruth would be enough.

“I understand that you were up at the cottage yesterday around the time the cottage was set on fire?” Susie asked, trying to catch the young woman out before she could throw up all her defences.

"What? How did you know that?" The shock was plain to see on her features.

"I can't actually reveal my source, but it is true, isn't it?"

"Well you already know it is. No crime in going for a walk is there?" Frannie answered wearily.

"Not unless you had something to do with the arson attack," Susie tried to throw Frannie off balance.

"What? I don't know what you mean." Frannie closed her eyes then rubbed at her temples. She wished the woman would just go away, yet didn't wish to make a scene and bring more attention to herself.

Susie could tell that she was hiding something, as much by her expression as her answer. "I think you do."

"Are you accusing me of something?" Frannie became more defensive.

"I'm sorry, but it is my job to ask these sorts of questions," Susie tried another tact, "You were with the two women that are now deceased, is that correct?"

Frannie shook her head as if to clear it, “Yes but…” She was lost for anything else to say.

“Who was it that set the fire, was it one of the other women?”

“No, I mean I don’t know what you’re going on about,” Frannie felt tears threatening.

“So, if it wasn’t one of them then it must have been you,” Susie said, hoping to bluff the young woman into spilling the beans.

“You don’t understand, you can’t,” whimpered Frannie. She couldn’t take any more, she just wanted it to go away, but knew that it wasn’t likely to. She knew if the policemen had pressed a little harder that she would have told them everything, and now knew that it was pointless to try and lie anymore, that it was all gong to come out.

“You could try me, I might,” Susie said hopefully.

“You’d think I was mad.” Frannie felt defeated, wash out and lost. “Where do I start? I don’t know.” She looked at Susie with a lost little girl look.

“At the start would be a good place,” Susie said, hiding the triumph she felt inside. Hoping to appear like someone you could tell anything.

“Well,” Frannie began after a moment. Before she knew it she was spilling all that had happened since that day after Micky’s funeral. By the end she was exhausted, yet glad it was over. She had felt so alone, with no-one to talk to about what had happened. Even her families’ visit had not eased her of the burden of what she knew. How could she explain it to anybody? She hadn’t known, not until pressed by Susie.

No sooner than telling the woman her tale and she began to think maybe she had said too much. She was a stranger after all, and was sure to make this into a story for her newspaper, which in turn would surely bring the police down on her for her part in the fire. She had the foresight not to admit to being the one who had thrown the fire bomb. Instead she had blamed Mandy for that. After all she hadn’t really known Mandy, and it had been her idea. She had been too close to Alice to lay the blame with her.

“I find this a little hard to believe,” Susie said, looking at the woman in the bed closely, “Why isn’t there more known about this?”

“I don’t know, but it’s real. I know because it tried to get at me, but somehow my baby saved me,” Frannie tried to sound convincing, yet doubted that Susie believed her.

“Why do you think that you failed to drive this…” She paused for effect, “Banshee back to the abyss?”

“I don’t know. It was Mandy that knew all about it. I wasn’t even sure it was real till it came to my house,” Frannie said demurely, shaking her head. She wiped a tear from her cheek.

“So why did you go along with the plan?”

“I thought I could talk them out of it,” She said. Well at least that was true to a point, she thought.

“You said Mandy remembered what had happened when she was younger,” Susie said, “But why didn’t she act sooner?”

“She said it wasn’t until Micky’s death that she realised that she needed to do something to stop it.”

Susie could see she had gotten as much as she could from the girl. What she was going to do with the information she was not quite sure. It would make a good story, though maybe not for a newspaper like the Standard, but it was better than no paper at all. “Well, thank you for speaking to me I will need to be going now, will you be okay?” She asked, more because she felt she should than from true concern.

“Yes, I be fine thanks,” Frannie said, sounding unconvincing.

Susie ignored the uncertainty.

“What will happen now?” Frannie asked, dreading the answer.

“I’m not sure, but I’ll try to leave you out of it if I can.” Susie didn’t see it would do any good to her article to mention Frannie’s, or the others’ part in the fire. If anything, by not mentioning how the fire was set would add to the story. She could see that this was a relief to the young woman.

“Well, thank you again,” she said, rising turning to leave. She patted Frannie on the shoulder to offer a little comfort before she left. She looked through the glass that separated the central corridor to the wards, but Frannie didn't look up to see her go, too busy wiping tears from her eyes. She felt a twinge of sympathy for her.

Susie wondered how much the girl had been telling the truth. She was sure that the girl hadn't told her the whole facts to what had happened, but most of what she had said had sounded as if she believed that the banshee was real. The idea of something so malicious though was hard to take as true. How could it be? She thought. Still the girl had thought it real. Still there were all the deaths associated with the old cottage, never mind the two women after trying to destroy the place.

She headed for the elevators, brimming with a building excitement. She was sure that she had learned more than what Munroe knew about his case. This knowledge pleased her. She smiled to herself as the lift doors closed.

Chapter 18

Munroe found sleep hard to find. His mind was still playing over the events of the past couple of days, more so than he wished. No matter how much he tried to clear his mind of Alice's prediction that she too would soon be dead, it kept recurring when he had a quiet moment. Was it just the grief talking? He kept asking himself. Even with the preliminary results from the coroner saying that Mandy's death was natural causes, it did nothing to shift it from his mind.

Finally as dawn began to creep over the horizon, he drifted into an uneasy sleep. With it he found himself in a strange dream where he was at the old cottage. The odd thing was that it hadn't been destroyed by the blaze. He stood in front of it watching as a girl, dressed in old style clothing, tended to the garden. She seemed unaware of his presence.

Why was this so strange? It was the middle of the night, and yet he could see clearly as if it were day. And the girl though working hard, seemed never to achieve anything. Other than her hands moving to pull the weeds from between the plants, she never moved along the rows she sat in the middle of.

He moved towards her, hoping to ask her why she seemed so intent on this single patch. As he did she looked up as he closed the short distance separating them. He stopped at the fence line but found when he tried to speak that he couldn't.

"Something wrong?" The girl asked, her voice was old, ragged and didn't seem to belong to her. When he still didn't reply she gave a short, chilly laugh as if to mock him. "Oh, maybe you've come to join my friends, is that it? You've come so I can put you in my jar." As she said this she lifted a large glass jar from the soil behind her, and held it up to him.

He looked at the jar as fear rose within him. But it was only a jar, he tried to tell himself. Yet there was something about that jar he didn't like. Was it the way it seemed to glow, and swirl with that greenish light as if it contained something radioactive. He wasn't sure. All he knew was he didn't want to get any closer to it.

As he drew his stare back to the girl the air filled with an ungodly scream. He saw that it came from her, and she was rising from her place on the ground. As she did her flesh seemed to melt from her features. The sight of her dissolving face brought more terror, yet he found himself rooted to the spot, unable to do anything other than wait for the creature to bring her jar to him.

He awoke with a start. Sweat dampened his forehead as well as the back of his neck. He rubbed at his gritty eyes. As they came to focus in the half light, which the curtains allowed in to the room, he thought he saw movement. He pushed himself up in the bed as he focused on a figure at the end of the bed. The fear from the dream still fresh in his mind, and irrationally, for an instant, he was sure that the creature was there with him in his room. He forced himself to get a grip.

"What the blazes? Who are you, and how did you get in here?" He demanded.

"I'm so sorry to frighten you like this inspector," Alice said, coming into view before settling on the edge of the bed.

A chill ran down Munroe's back, as much from the chill in the air as the sight of the woman that had died days before. He was sure that he must still be trapped in the dream. "But you…"

"I know, not to worry though," she sounded cheery, "but I did say that I might see you again, didn't I?"

"But how?"

"There are as many things unseen as there are visible to the living," she answered.

"I don't understand."

"Here take this it will help keep you safe," Alice said, extending her hand out to Munroe. A small silver cross dangled from a chain.

Munroe took it with a questioning look, but said nothing.

"You know what you have to do, you have to end the horror," she explained, "Your friend the reporter will help."

“Who?” He shook his head trying to make sense of the surreal nature of the situation, “You can’t mean Susie McLean?”

“Of course I do, who else is there?” She smiled as if she were explaining something to a child, “Find the jar and free those she has trapped within. You have to do it, or she’ll add Susie to those she has already taken. It’s up to you to end this, you understand?”

“Yes,” he said, but really he was struggling with what she was saying. “Why can’t you?”

“If I could I would, now take this,” she said still holding out the cross.

He took it, letting the chain dangle across the back of his hand. The cross hidden in his enclosed palm. “Why me?”

“Who else could I ask?” She questioned, though she didn’t wait for his reply, “Now you need to get some sleep.”

He obeyed, not knowing why, sliding down in the bed. His eyelids suddenly feeling too heavy to remain open and close like shutters. He tried to force them open to look at Alice. He wanted to ask her something, yet didn’t know what. His eyes remained closed though, and sleep snatched him in its grip before he had a chance to fight it.

He was awoken by his alarm clocks demands to get up. As he reached out to slap it quiet the chain fell on his bedside table. As silence was returned to the room, he looked at the cross. He lifted it from where it had come to lie, fingering it in his hand as the memory of his visitor came back. With it, pieces of the earlier dream also surfaced. He gave a shiver.

If Alice was a dream, then how the heck did I get this? He questioned himself. And what was it she said? I have to end it, that I would know how? But I don't. He rubbed at his face, as much to clear his mind of the racing thoughts within, as to clear the sleep from his grainy eyes. "Find the jar, but where?" He asked under his breath, though he already knew the answer, or at least he was sure where to look. The cottage.

* * *

Susie looked at the pictures on the monitor and huffed to herself. It wasn't that they were bad, but they certainly weren't to the quality that her editor would like. Being a small local rag meant that often she had to provide pictures for the stories she covered, unfortunately it wasn't one of her strong points.

She dreaded the thought of going back to the woods to get more pictures, yet could see no other way. The nightmare she had during the night made it feel like a dark proposition. She'd been trapped in the cellar, and could sense something was with her, something that had a darkness to it. As she tried to reach the stairs they had collapsed, trapping her. It was then that the apparition had appeared. A ghastly disfigured being with the cold white eyes of a boiled fish, and smelled of putrefying death. As it had reach out for her she had screamed out in fear as she tried to back away from the creature. It was then that she had sat bolt upright, wide awake and covered in sweat.

As she looked at the screen again, the dream still clung to her consciousness. It sent a shiver of apprehension down her spine. "No you're just being silly," she told herself, yet she found it hard to shake. She closed the file containing the photos to reveal the story she had spent much of the previous evening writing. The headline screamed out to her, “Fire At Haunted House.” She felt satisfied with it as she knew it would grab punters eyes. She hoped to see her story on the cover, but she needed the right picture. It was a pity she hadn’t gotten to the cottage while the fire brigade had been fighting the blaze. That sort shot would have been worth a story on its own.

She checked the time at the bottom right of the screen and saw she was running late. She quickly sent her story to her office computer, before powering the system down. One last check was made to be sure that everything was in its place, then she grabbed her jacket from the hall as she left for the office.

“Susie,” Her boss beckoned as she entered the office half an hour later.

“Yeah,” she approached wearily.

“Can you cover for Lou at the court this morning, he phoned in with a dodgy belly. He was out last night at some do or other and says he must have eaten something dodgy. More than likely he just had too much to drink, and is now suffering for his over indulgence."

"You don't mean for the whole day?" She didn't like the idea of hanging around the court house for the whole day just because Lou had got drunk the night before, even if this was the first time he had done so when he had work the next day.

"Well it would make my job easier," her editor pleaded, though one look told him it wasn't working, "okay, okay, just for this morning, I see if Jill can take over this afternoon."

"Well since you're so charming, but I have things to do later, so don't forget to get Jill or you'll have no-one covering the court, not that it would be a big loss."

"I said I'd get her and I will. Now off you go, and give us some news," he said, ushering her on her way.

She wasn't happy with having to delay her planned visit to get the pictures she needed, yet contented herself that she would at least still have the afternoon to travel up the valley to get the snaps for her story.

Chapter 19

Susie checked in at the clerk's desk after reaching the court building. Showing her press ID to gain a list of cases being heard in court that morning she made her way back to the main entrance. Her editor hadn't said anything about any particular case he wanted covering, so she took it as just a basic fishing exercise. She hadn't thought to check her colleague's desk to see if he had left any notes on anything he might have been following either.

As she looked down the list she noticed the arresting officers names related to the cases. Munroe's name caught her attention. She decided to sit in on this in the hope of seeing her favourite CID man. She looked forward to him being called, just so she could get a good look of his behind if nothing else. She glanced around guiltily at the thought. She looked at the charge the defendants were up for, and noticed that he must have made a break in the burglaries he was investigating. He would be eager to see those responsible in front of the judge. And who knows he might be a little more forthcoming about his other cases, she thought.

She soon found her target. “Inspector Munroe, glad to see you again.”

“Miss McLean, what brings you to the court? I hope you’ve not found yourself in any trouble?”

“Just doing my job,” she answered his sarcasm.

“I see, so you’re covering the court these days. Isn’t that a bit of a step down for you?” He asked distractedly.

“Just for one morning, covering a sick colleague,” she smiled as if not noticing Munroe’s offhandedness.

“So is there something I could help you with?”

“I see you have an interest in a case concerning a burglary. Is this anything to do with those happening up in the valley?”

“That would be correct, but you’ll hear all about it in the court room,” Munroe said dryly. Just then the court room doors were opened by the court clerk to admit the crowd. Munroe signalled Susie to go first.

"So, no news on the cause of Mrs. Brown's death?" She inquired, as they took a seat.

"Not as yet, but I'm sure you'll hear when I do."

"Any clues on the fire at the cottage?"

"So far our inquiries have drawn nothing, but the thinking is that it was local youths, as I have already told you previously," he said impatiently. He found questions over old ground tedious though it was something he himself did a lot in his job.

"So you aren't looking at Mrs. Brown, and her sister having any connection to it?"

Munroe looked at her hard, wondering what she knew. Had she visited Frannie at the hospital? He wondered. "Have you some information that may suggest that I should?"

"No," she lied, not wishing to share her story till she had it in print. "If I find out though, you'll be the second to know after my editor, I'm sure."

“Silence in the court!” The call to order echoed through the court room, bringing an end to the chitter chatter.

Once the judge had entered, and found his place Susie pulled out her note book. Munroe watched her, still wondering what she knew. He hoped that Frannie hadn’t opened up to the reporter. He knew if she had the Susie would surely use it in a story, leaving him nothing left to do than cause the girl more hardship. He hoped that if Frannie had said something that Susie would have the heart to see the trouble the girl would be in. That she had suffered enough difficult circumstances recently to deserve a break.

* * *

Munroe had been glad when the case had finally been heard. He was disappointed when the two lads had gotten bailed to appear at a later date, though it wasn’t unexpected given the overcrowding in the jails. He’d had to wait till after the midmorning break, which kept him longer at the courts than he would have liked.

Susie had made the most of it though to try to get any glimmer of information for her story. Though he had been alarmed to learn that she was going back to the cottage that afternoon he hid his concerns, not wishing to discuss the dream, or his ghostly visitor. He knew that he would have to find the time to make sure that the reporter came to no harm. He was sure now that his caller had been real. He wished Alice hadn't popped into see him with her dire warnings. It made him think back to his interview with Ferris, and question what was real. Could there really be an evil spirit in the cottage? But if there were good spirits like Alice, then there had to be evil ones.

After court he had to drop into the station for a time to do more paperwork. Just dotting the i's concerning his visit to court. A waste of his time he thought, but it had to be done to keep the politicians happy. With it the remains of the morning slide away before he noticed. A growl from his empty stomach telling him it was needing filling and soon.

When he realised Johnson was away on other duties whilst he was in court, he found himself doing his great disappearing act again. After getting food he headed up the valley, stuffing his face as he drove.

As he drove along the rutted trackway he was filled with a growing sense that something was wrong, yet tried hard to ignore it. Ahead the charred remains of the cottage appeared to the side. He felt relieved to see no other cars waiting there, it gave him strength to push the dread down. Maybe she isn't coming after all, he hoped silently. He pulled the car into the side before making the awkward manoeuvres to get his car facing back to the theme park. He killed the engine to wait, while he ate his lunch, hoping that it was in vain.

Munroe looked over the walls; black soot stained the opening that remained of the lower window, and door, like ghostly fingers of the flames that had ravaged the dwelling. He could still see charred beams sticking into the air from the rear wall, leaning awkwardly. Through the open doorway he noticed that the kitchen at the back was still intact. He wondered about the jar, could it be there. It seemed likely to him but he refrained from getting out of the car to investigate. Even in the bright sunlight the place gave an eerie feel.

Munroe was just thinking about going when he saw a glint in the distance. It took form as a familiar car approaching. He stayed in the car till the other, containing the reporter came to a stopped just as it had on the day of the fire. He could see that Susie was surprised to see him there waiting for her.

Susie got out of her vehicle, composing herself as she did. “Detective, I didn’t expect to see you again so soon or here for that matter,” she said, as if it were a question on approaching his car.

“Well you said you were coming up to the cottage, and I didn’t like the idea of you having an accident, so I thought I best check, but I seem to have gotten here early.” He lied, hoping it sound like a good one.

She seemed genuinely taken aback, and uncertain of what to say at first. “Well, I’m only here to get a few photos. I’m sure that shouldn’t put me in any danger, unless you think that there is something to the old myth surrounding this place," she indicated the ruin with her thumb.

"What?" He gave her a mask of astonishment to hide his thoughts inside, "And I suppose you do?"

"Well," she began, "what is it you detectives always say, when ever you eliminate the impossible and all that."

"And that would leave us with what? And wasn't that Sherlock Holmes?"

"Whatever. For me, some pictures for my piece on the fire are all I need," she said not wishing to think beyond her job. She headed back to her car, and reached into the back to retrieve an expensive looking digital SLR camera.

"Didn't you get enough the other day?" He asked, opening his door.

"They didn't turn out as well as I thought," she answered wearily. "So you only came out here to make sure that I wouldn't have a fall, and hurt myself, that was very thoughtful of you."

"I wouldn't like to think that something bad might happen to you, especially here. The gossips would have a field day."

"I'm sure they would," Susie conceded, feeling secretly pleased at his concern. She moved to the side and took her first picture, checking it on the back screen, and looked unhappily at it.

"Maybe you could try getting lower down, I've heard that is good for building shots," Munroe suggested.

Susie gave him a look of appreciation, but said nothing. She did however take his advice for the next few shots. She looked pleased at the result, yet still refrained from thanking the policeman.

"Do you think it would be safe to try, and get some pictures from inside?" Susie asked, breaking the silence.

Munroe had been pretending to ignore her though kept glancing from the side of his eyes. He now looked round trying hard to look thoughtful. "I'm sure it should be, but I'm coming just in case as I don't like the look of those rafters up there."

"Do you think that I can't manage on my own?" She ignored looking at the danger he had mentioned.

"Not at all, but I like sometimes to check a place out again; after all it is always good to have second look around a scene, you can never tell what was missed the first time," Munroe lied again with a more convincing smile, knowing this was a better untruth than the last one.

"Really," Susie smiled, but didn't reveal she knew he was just giving her a line, "well it's nice to know the police are always there when in need."

She didn't wait for him to reply. She stopped at the doorway regretting her idea on seeing the blackened interior. She only moved inside when she felt Munroe at her back, not wishing to hear him commenting on her hesitation. She looked around at the remains of dividing walls, now blackened skeletons.

"It must have been quite a nice little house at one time," Munroe said wistfully.

"A bit small though," Susie added.

"Cosy I'd say."

“Mmm,” Susie grudgingly agreed, as she clicked another shot before moving further into the remains. “It looks like the back has survived,” She noted more to herself.

“Yeah, I think it’s some sort of extension,” Munroe stated.

“Looks as old as the rest,” Susie said, studying stone walls as she entered the kitchen. Light flood in from the broken windows, evidence of the firemen’s visit. Beyond the view was of a neglected, overgrown garden being slowly reclaimed by the woods surrounding it.

“Strange this floor is wooden,” noted Munroe.

Susie looked down at the floor before glancing at Munroe, then past him. “Is that a door?”

Munroe looked over his shoulder at the partially hidden door. “Yes, never noticed that last time I was here,” he said, pushing the kitchen door closed to get a better look at the one it had been hiding.

“You think it goes anywhere?” She hoped that it was just a cupboard or pantry as the memory of her nightmare suddenly surfacing in the back of her mind. She watched as Munroe twisted the handle, releasing the door. It pushed inward creakily, revealing stairs down into a cellar. She gave a shiver.

"I'll go get my torch, you can wait here if you want."

"Your not going down there, are you?" She asked fearfully, trying not to show her apprehension.

"Why not?"

"No reason," Susie replied, hoping to appear unconcerned.

"Be back in a minute," he said with a smile and quickly disappeared on his errand.

Susie stared at the crack of darkness left uncovered by the door to the rest of the house being open again. She looked around the small room noticing the pump handle over the old sink, still showing white. In a corner stood a rust range cooker, she guessed was a wood burner. She wondered why someone hadn't made off with it as she knew they could fetch a good price. She turned towards the door as she heard Munroe returning.

“Here we go,” he said, flipping the torch on and off to be sure it worked.

“Are you sure the stairs will be safe?” She asked as she crossed the room.

“One way to find out,” he answered cheerfully, though he didn’t feel as happy as he sounded. At that he turned through the door and began to descend into the darkness, cutting his way through with the light of the torch.

Susie followed, she gave a shiver at the chill the air held coming from below. A little daylight managed to claim a small hold near the top of the stairway but failed in getting beyond the fist couple of steps. As she followed Munroe down the stairs creaked, making her nervous. Only as she reached the small square landing half way down, where the stairs turned did the stairs stop protesting at being subjected to the passage of the visitors. She watched the light swing in a great arc around the small cellar as Munroe reach the bottom.

“Not much to see,” he said, sounding a little disappointed.

“What were you expecting?” Her eyes now adjusting, she was amazed at the amount of light the torch gave. She felt a chill as she realised she was in a room not unlike the one from her dream.

“Not sure,” he replied under his breath. He looked at the wall that supported the stairs. “Shouldn’t there be a door under the stairs?”

“What?” She gazed to where he indicated but said nothing else.

Munroe moved to the wooden wall examining it, his policeman’s instincts taking control. He noticed a cross like shadow on the dirty wood and beside this it looked as if the wood had rotted. As he reached out to touch the panelling his torch blinked on and off. He gave it a shake which seemed to work.

“I think I’ve seen enough,” Susie said, retreating up the stairs.

“Not frightened of the dark are you?” He asked in a playful manner.

“No,” she replied, stopping on the stairs half way up, just beyond the small landing to turn to let Monroe see she was in command of herself. Her gaze had hardly fallen on him when she found herself falling through the stairs as they gave under her. As she landed her finger pressed the button on the camera hang from her neck. The flash blinded her, and she was sure the scream was somehow coming from herself as she tried to blink away the temporary blindness.

Munroe carefully ascended the stairs to the collapse, not wishing to join Susie. As he reached the lip of the hole a fearful sound met his ears. His mouth dried and he had to fight to force his vocal chords to work. "Susie, Susie, are you okay," he whispered into the gap. Unnoticed a ghostly figure had been thrown by the blinding light into the main cellar.

"Yes, I think so," Susie answered, coughing a little at the dust slowly settling in the confined space. She tried to brush herself down.

"Move over and I'll come down," Munroe said, preparing to drop down to where Susie stood.

"Can't you just pull me up?"

"I'm not sure if the stairs will take both our weight," he said, with half an ear on the further protests the stairs were making under him. He handed Susie the torch and began to lower himself into the cupboard.

"How are we going to get out?" Susie wondered aloud. The torch began to blink again. Susie shook it but it continued to strobe.

"How dare you?"

They looked round as one at the figure standing a few short feet from them. "Who?" Munroe asked, shaken by the unexpected confrontation.

"How?" Susie added her own confused question.

"As if you don't already know, coming here," the banshee said angrily.

As the apparition began her change, Susie's fingers found the button on her camera again. The screams of the banshee were clear through the momentary blindness that ensued. As Munroe found his vision returning, he felt relief that the figure was gone. At the same moment his eyes settled on an old jar sitting on a stone shelf, like the wine on an alter and a chill played up his spine, raising the hairs on the back of his neck.

The banshee vented her rage into the dark cellar beyond the wall. Munroe stepped in front of Susie protectively, feeling the cross that Alice had left him. He hadn't known why he was wearing it but felt glad that he could feel it under his shirt. The air filled with the smell of rotting burnt flesh as the creature reappeared inches from Munroe. It reached out for his chest but as its hand touched him, he watched in stunned silence as it recoiled as if hit by a bolt of lightning.

"Quick, smash the jar," Munroe told Susie, forcefully.

She was frozen for a moment as the chilling screams of anger fill the air once more. Munroe nudged her but she found herself just looking dumbly at him for what seemed like an age. She retreated as the horror returned. It stood between them and the cold stone holding the glass container.

Munroe thought fast as the thing looked malevolently at them. "Close your eyes and use the camera," he ordered.

Susie took a moment to take the command in, before depressing the switch again. She didn't close her eyes as Munroe had, so stood blind as the creature was force to flea the burning light. Munroe saw the flash through his closed eyes and opened them, before moved with purpose towards the jar in two large strides. He grasped as the panic stricken creature return, sensing what the man had in mind.

"Noooo," it screeched, as it watched the jar being raised over Munroe's head. With more force than he really required he hurled it onto the shelf. It exploded releasing the vilest stench Munroe, or Susie had ever experienced. Their eyes watered as the torch failed completely. In the gloom that enveloped them they watched fairy lights rising into the air.

"Why did you do that?" Whimpered the banshee, a shadow of what she was, her power now drained with the loss of her captives. "I was punishing the wrong doers." The words were more of a whimper than anything else.

Munroe was dumbfounded by the spectre's statement. He was not expecting the sudden flush of anger that gave strength renewed to the banshee. As she felt the power reach its peak, she wailed fearlessly at the transgressors. As she reached out to seek revenge against

Susie, the reporter used her camera to defend herself from the enraged being.

The force of the blinding light threw the now solid form of the banshee back. She struck the door that had been hidden from the other side of the wall. It gave easily, coming cleanly from the old decayed hinges and broke the rotted wood from the walls. The cellar beyond was lit by a strange golden light, which the banshee at first did not notice. The last of her power was now gone, leaving her no more than a bitter shadow remonstrating the injustice she had suffer, of her mission.

Munroe and Susie moved to stand in the doorway now uncovered. They watched, unable to speak as the light grew brighter. The fairy lights they had gazed at moments before took on human form. Amongst them Munroe was sure he saw Mandy, she seemed to turn to look at him, with a smile. Then she was gone.

As the cellar cleared of its ghostly host, another figure appeared. Munroe stood spell bound as did Susie. They could clearly see that the man was dressed in the garb of a preacher from over two hundred years ago. He took a few steps to where the banshee sat, clutching her knees like an unhappy little girl.

"Oh, my poor Helen," the man said with great sorrow.

"I was only punishing the wrong doers," she said, barely looking at the new arrival.

"Well now it is time that you leave this world my poor dear Helen," he said concern easily visible to the spectators.

"But I can't," Helen said, fearful of what would now become of her.

"You have no choice, it is time for you to come with me," the words were said with a gentle kindness, yet were so compelling that the banshee could not resist. She rose, taking the minister's offered hand and was led away. Both those watching had no doubt that the creature was gone.

The golden light faded, with it the torches light returned at full brightness until it was all that lit the cellar. Still the pair stood, too stunned to move or say anything. Finally Munroe moved from the doorway, flashing the light around into the corners as if searching.

“What the heck just happened?” Susie asked, finding her voice.

“What ever it was, I think its over,” he said with a great sense of relief.

“Was that the thing Ferris told me about?”

“I have no idea,” Munroe replied, yet guessed that it was indeed the same thing the man in question had said lived in the cottage.

“How did you know to break that jar?” It had just struck Susie what Munroe had done and was sure that was what Ferris had meant by the object holding the banshee to this realm. But how had Munroe known?

“A lucky guess,” he ventured hopefully, “Anyway we should get out of here now. Got any ideas?”

“We could use this door,” Susie suggested, standing on it to check to see how it felt. It seemed to be still sturdy as it had been protected from the ravages of time by the wall that had been built in front of it. She stepped off of it, satisfied.

Munroe flashed the light onto it and looked intently. “Looks good, here take the torch.” He hand the light to Susie, before stooping to heft the door up. It was heavier than he had thought, yet managed to get it over the hole in the stairs. Once in place he took the torch back and aided Susie. The stairs creaked threateningly, giving Munroe a moment's hesitation.

As they left the ruins, heading for their cars Susie turned to the policeman, "You wouldn't like to give me a statement about what just happened?"

"No, sorry I have no idea what just happened," he stated, at that his phone buzzed noisily in his jacket pocket. "Yes, Munroe," he said into it, "Yeah, I'm just grabbing some lunch will be there in ten, okay."

"Nothing important, I hope," Susie said, still hopeful that Munroe might give her something for her new story that was forming in her head.

"Sorry, I can't. I have a career to think of." At that he turned for his car.

Susie stood for a moment before turning to her own vehicle, leaving the old cottage to fall back into the local legend. That night she found the picture for her story but as she checked the random shots of when she had been trapped with Munroe, she was saddened not to find one that she could use as proof of what had happened in the cellar.

It would have made a great story, she thought to herself. She closed her computer down, her bed calling to her as tiredness gritted her eyes.

Epilogue

Ba-boom, ba-boom. The sound reassures me all is well. I take comfort from the knowledge that the sound is the beat of my new mother's heart. A loving heart I am sure. She will love me and this new chance of a happy life will give me the chance to live a good life. One removed from the past existence of seeking revenge.

Ba-boom, ba-boom, ba-boom. I can hear the beat speeding in tempo. Is something wrong? I don't feel the joy that usually fills me when my mum is happy. Instead there is something frightening about this beat. What?

Ba-boom, ba-boom, ba-boom, ba-boom. I know there is something wrong now. I don't know what but I'm sure of it. My heart is racing too, yet what can I do as I float about in here? I want to make it right. I want to hear that steady beat, slow and steady, reassuring.

Silence. No it can't be. Mum, where are you. You can't just stop. I have still to be born. I need to be born. I have to wash the old away with the new life promised to me. Please don't leave me, please.

I feel my life ending before I had a chance to take a breath. What cruelty. Who could do this? Who could take the life of an unborn? Or silence the heart of a mother still carrying her young.

I rise into the world and remember those that I had judged and punished in my time as the banshee. I had called the curse down on the false accusers and reeked justice on them. Now I can feel that anger rising as I looked down on the woman that was to be my mother, washing away my former life. Her blood pools from her chest on the ground before her. Who has done this?

I see the light but I can't go. Not until I find justice for this crime against my would be mother. I searched the back street but there is no sign of the guilty. I know I will find them though and then…

www.ingramcontent.com/pod-product-compliance
Ingram Content Group UK Ltd.
Pitfield, Milton Keynes, MK11 3LW, UK
UKHW040602210726
13854UKWH00008B/1840

9 781447 525899